Writing on the Wall
Survival Series
Book One
By Tracey Ward

For woman who refuse

to be a Wendy.

Tracey Ward

Chapter One

It happened at Christmas. Quite a time for the world to end but if we could pick and choose when Hell unhinged its jaw and tried to swallow us whole we'd probably pick never.

As it is, I suppose it could have been worse. Being eight years old and watching your neighbor break through the sliding glass door like it was made of paper isn't the most traumatizing thing ever. His blood spurting from shredded wounds and dead vacant eyes that somehow still see you, *really* see you? You can come back from that. After a few weeks I'd even get over the black blood that dripped onto my brand new Cabbage Patch Doll with the blond hair and pretty, smiling eyes. It's fine. That's all fine.

What you don't come back from is watching him eat your parents. Literally, honestly, violently eat your parents. I saw it. All of it. Huddled behind the Christmas tree, peaking out through the fragrant green needles and soft glow of the multicolored lights, I watched it happen. And I remember. The sounds, the sight, the smell. I'll never forget. Nearly ten years later I can relive it with perfect clarity but I seriously try not to. Life is horrifying enough. I don't need to borrow on past troubles.

Today my trouble is a wolf. Have wolves ever really been an issue in downtown Seattle before? I don't know. I was just a kid when crazy came to town but I'm willing to bet not. They're everywhere now. A lot of animals are. The city has become a wilderness in a whole new way. Used to be you had to worry about walking alone at night because you might get jumped by a member of a gang or a desperate soul pushed to the limit. Now you have to worry about getting jumped by an animal in a pack or a starving zombie desperate for your brain, not your wallet. There really aren't that many of them left anymore, though. I mean, they're around, don't be fooled and don't be stupid. I'm just saying it's not like it was. Not like in the beginning. But right now I'm pretty sure the wolves outnumber the dead.

This one is a dark gray color, long and lithe. He'd be pretty if he weren't so deadly. Also if he weren't in my way. I need to go out to get fresh water from one of the rain traps I've set up on other buildings farther out. I make sure to never do it on my own building aside from one small hidden bucket for emergencies. It's about half full but I'm thirsty and it's getting late.

I'm standing in the dark entryway of my building watching the animal wander the street, sniffing the knee high grass growing through cracks in the asphalt. The roads are a mess these days. Really makes me wonder where our tax dollars are going. I'm just about to make a break for it when I catch movement in another doorway farther down the street. I freeze, waiting and watching, barely breathing. It moves again, too tall to be an animal and too precise to be a zombie. It's another person. This bothers me more than anything else. I shrink back farther into the shadows, making sure I'm completely hidden, and I watch to see what the guy's plan is.

I know it's a man. Not from any details of his outline or instinct or scent on the wind. I know it because statistically it's probably true. There aren't many women out here in the wild, not anymore. Most of us either died or entered the Colonies, of which there are too many if you ask me. There are several spread all over the city with hundreds of people in each one. It sounds like a great way to spread the virus some more. Really bring on the second coming. I'm one of the few people, male or female, doing it alone and being a woman on the outside is not ideal. In fact it's downright dangerous. Some of us can't make it. There are a lot of predators out here and odds are one of them will get you eventually.

Numbers don't lie.

So that's how I just know this shadow messing with my plans is a guy. Probably part of a pack of his own, the thought of which makes me drop yet another step back into my building. I'm a girl stuck in Neverland with The Lost Boys. I'm no Wendy, I can hold my own. I don't need to wait around for Peter to save me but I'm also not an idiot. I know my enemies.

After what feels like forever he finally makes his move. The shadow rushes quickly and surprisingly stealthily through the tangle of weeds, grass and ravaged cars until he's directly behind the animal. I shake my head at how utterly stupid a move this is. You're about to see why.

The wind shifts. The wolf smells him and he's on alert, his haunches going up, his teeth becoming exposed. He turns slowly toward the guy. There's a long tense moment while they watch each other, neither moving a single muscle. My own muscles ache just from watching and I realize that I'm crouched down, either ready to fight or spring into a sprint.

Fight or flight. I think. *Come on, guy, what's it going to be?*

Color me every shade of the rainbow surprised when he picks fight. He's either crazy brave or just plain crazy. As he runs at the wolf I catch a glint of steel flash against the failing light of the day. He's got a knife. It better be pretty big and he better be unbelievably fast with it. I'm trying to sort out why he would even attack this animal in the first place when they collide. The wolf snarls as the guy grunts, then they hit the ground and I can't see them anymore. Now would be a spectacular time for me to get out of here. To either go upstairs, lay low and make do with my emergency water rations or head for the hills to find more.

I'm scanning the sidewalk, surprised it's still clear, and leaning toward the water idea when the guy cries out in agony. The sound makes me cringe. I instantly hate myself for it. You learn not to empathize here in this mad new world. Sympathy will only get you killed. But something about the sound gets to me and I hesitate. He's going to lose. He is going to die and the wolf is alone, meaning he won't eat all of him. Either many more wolves will be here helping him feast when I get back, this guy's buddies will be here cleaning up the mess of his desecrated body or the infected will have descended. No matter how you slice it, if he dies on my front porch like this, I'm not making it back in this building tonight. And with the possibility of Lost Boys this close to home, I probably won't ever return.

I swear under my breath, thoroughly pissed off. But I'm also trapped. I have to either do something or go back inside and be prepared to wait it out. Without water that's going to suck. So I do the one thing I really do not want to do.

I save a man's life.

I reluctantly pull out my knife as I silently close the distance between myself, animal and idiot. From a distance I thought the wolf was pretty but up close it's beautiful. It makes me even angrier that I have to do this. There's not much beauty left in the world, I'd rather leave it when I can find it. Like walking around a flower somehow blooming in the broken pavement of a desolate road.

I roll up on the wolf in his blind spot, his eye covered by the guy's one good hand that's trying desperately to keep dripping, gnashing teeth out of his jugular. It strikes me that it doesn't look that much different from fighting a Risen. His other arm is a bloody mess pressed against the animal's chest, coating his fur in red.

When I'm within striking range I slash at the wolf's side. My knife goes in easy because if I do anything in this world right it's keep my weapons deadly. But I make sure not to sink the blade in too deeply. I've decided I won't kill it, a decision that is incredibly stupid but one I can sleep with tonight. I don't want to kill it. I want it to keep running its patrols with its pack keeping infected and Lost Boys at bay. I've only grazed it, only grabbed its attention, and even though it's probably a really bad choice, I don't regret it. Not yet anyway.

The animal leaps off the guy then turns to face me,

seeing me as the new threat.

"Get up," I tell the body on the ground, never looking away from the wolf. "Slowly."

He does as I say and I'm surprised when he does it silently. I expected groaning and moaning, maybe even ungrateful proclamations of his ability to handle it himself. Had he done that I wouldn't have hesitated to let the animal have him. But he gets up and comes to stand beside me, his knife at the ready in his uninjured hand.

"Get out of here," I tell him, my voice low and soothing for the wolf's sake.

"No way," he replies quietly.

"I wasn't asking. Go."

"No."

I'm shaking mad now. His blood is dripping onto the pavement at an alarming rate. I'm doing the math in my head figuring how fast that crimson pool will bring the infected. Not long now.

"Get out of here. NOW," I grind out through gritted teeth.

The wolf takes an angry step forward, the low vibration of his growl standing the hair on my arms on end.

"Not until he's dead."

"Seriously?" I whisper incredulously. I shift my knife in my sweating palm. "You want wolf for dinner that bad?"

"I want revenge that bad."

"This is for revenge?" I ask, feeling shocked. "On a wolf?"

"He killed my brother."

"Unbelievable."

I should have let him die.

I begin to back away from him and the animal, making my way slowly toward the sidewalk. They can sort this out together. I'm heading to one of my buildings with a water source. I'll camp out there tonight and find a new home tomorrow. I hate it but with all this blood out front and him knowing where I live, no matter who wins this fight I'm the loser out of a home.

I hate people more than ever and I like animals a lot less too.

"Where are you going?" he whispers.

The wolf is advancing, empowered by my retreat.

"If you won't leave, I will. Good luck with this. You're gonna die.'

Before I can make it two steps, low growls emanate from up and down the street. I spot dark, lean wolves advancing on us from out of the growing shadows. So far I count six. Three each, he's down a hand and he couldn't even handle one at full strength. Now we're both gonna die.

The guy curses, stepping back in line with me.

I chuckle bitterly. "Yeah."

"We need to run. We can't fight them all off."

"We can't outrun them all either."

"No."

"Back up. Keep backing up and head to the left. There's a doorway. That's where we're going."

He glances over his shoulder quickly, verifying that the way is clear.

"You've been in this building before?"

I nod sharply. "A time or two."

"There's a door close by that we can close on them?"

"Why else would I be taking us there?"

11

"Sorry if I don't trust the judgment of a total stranger."

I fight the urge to stab him. "You're really saying that to the girl who just saved your life? If I'd known you were *getting revenge*," I say, my voice dripping in sarcasm. "I would have happily watched you die."

"You have no idea what you're talking about."

"You have no idea what you're *doing*," I whisper viciously.

"I didn't ask you to help me," he nearly shouts, pissing me off further. "You didn't have to be part of this."

"No, but you needed help. And you made me part of this when you staged your Shakespearean drama at my front door."

He glances at the building behind us again, frowning. "This is where you—"

"Run!"

I shove him in the shoulder, launching us both in the direction of the door. When we take off running, the wolves fall in step behind us and they are *fast*. I'm not even sure we'll make it to the door unhurt. I quickly dart in front of the guy, making sure if they get ahold of anything it's his dumb ass.

We sprint over the cracked marble floors, the skitter of claws following close behind. I grab onto the door and begin to swing it closed behind me. And, no, I don't check to make sure he's going to make it. That's his issue, not mine.

He jumps to the side just as a wolf is lunging to take a bite out of his back. Good on him for keeping himself safe but that move leaves me wide open. Luckily I'm already shoving the door closed on the animals face. He rams into it, bouncing off harmlessly.

But the door isn't so much a door as it is a gate and when he lunges again he gets ahold of my coat. He jerks back on the fabric and I'm wrenched hard against the steel. I cry out in surprise and pain as my arm is twisted then pinned at a strange angle. The guy yanks me back, pulling me from the animal's clutches. I stumble against the wall as he releases me quickly to latch the door, barely snatching his fingers clear before they're bitten off.

"That was close," he says, breathing heavily.

He looks at me with a lopsided grin.

I punch him in the face. The sound of skin on skin and bone connecting through meat vibrates through the small space. It takes him by surprise, sending him stumbling back a step.

"What the—what is your problem?!" he cries, rubbing his cheek. His grin is gone.

"With you? I don't know where to begin! I've known you five minutes and you've almost gotten me killed twice!"

"How was this my fault?" he demands, gesturing to the snarling wolves and metal. "You said there was a door! This is not a door."

"It's not solid but it's still a door. It's keeping them out, isn't it?"

"I don't know, is it? Let's ask your coat."

He points to my sleeve. I look down to find the fleece ripped wide open.

"No, that's okay," I say sarcastically, glaring at him. "I have tons of clothes. I can afford to be missing a coat in the dead of winter."

"Sorry, princess, didn't mean to destroy your wardrobe," he mutters, glancing around.

We're deep in shadow but a small shaft of light is

coming through one of the broken windows giving me my first decent look at him. He's tall and lean with brown eyes and dark hair. He's about my age, seventeen, and clean shaven so he must have a home somewhere with some amenities. Some comforts. His clothes also look decently clean which means he has access to water and a safe place to wash. I peg him solidly then and there as part of a gang.

It doesn't mean what it used to. He's not a thug, at least I doubt he is. He's just a guy who signed up to be part of a group that helps each other survive. Kind of like the Colonies but less like a prison. It's another situation I can understand people entering into, it's just not for me. Especially since these gangs are almost all men.

His eyes land on me then and I'm annoyed that he caught me examining him. His brows crease together in confusion or annoyance. I wonder what he sees in me that makes him do it. I've looked in mirrors. I've seen old ads scattered around. I've even seen a few movies. I know what pretty is and I know I'm it; tall, thin (though that's out of my hands really, I'd be fat if I could be), dark red hair, fair skin, pale blue eyes. Guess I'm not his type, though in the end of days I'm surprised to find a teenage boy so picky.

And now I have to deal with him. Probably all night. He can't leave now and I can't hide where I live, not unless I want to stay in one of the empty, blown out rooms somewhere else in the building. Pretty much every room but mine is missing windows or a door. Not ideal living quarters, even for one night. Not in the cold of winter. Not with blood outside.

"Come on," I tell him grudgingly.

I lead him up the stairs as the wolves snarl and yap

angrily behind us. I flip them off over my shoulder. He falls in step behind me without a word and part of my animosity toward him slips. We walk up ten flights of stairs before I take us out of the stairwell into a hall. This is where I live, or *lived* before he came around to ruin everything. My animosity is instantly back. I lead him halfway down the hall where I open the door to the warehouse apartment I've called home for almost a year now. It's one of the first times I've actually gotten settled. I have more things in here than I can carry out on my back, a huge deal for me. Now I'll have to leave almost all of it behind.

As I hurry to light a couple of small candles for his sake (and the sake of my possessions I'd rather he didn't trample over) I glance over my shoulder to make sure he closes the door. He looks around, sees the board I use to barricade it and quickly slips it into the braces that cradle it horizontally. We are now as safe as two teenagers in a world full of zombies can be. I fuss over the ripped sleeve of my jacket but I'm watching him out of the corner of my eye as he takes in my place. He seems surprised by it. He should be. It took a lot of time and a lot of effort to get it this way.

"You live here alone," he says, not even trying to make it a question.

I snort. "I'm not exactly social."

"Shocking."

"Don't take it as an invitation. I can defend myself."

He looks over at me, his eyes surprised. "Never crossed my mind."

"Sure."

He shakes his head in disgust, looking away. "What's with the exercise bike? Don't get enough cardio running from the Risen?"

"I don't ride it for exercise. I ride it for fun."

"Yeah, you seem fun," he mutters, kneeling beside the bike to examine the wires trailing from it. They lead a short distance across the distressed floors over to a small generator. From there they lead up to— "Is that a laptop?" he asks incredulously.

I have to suppress a smile as I work to keep the pride out of my voice. "It's a portable TV/DVD player. Riding the bike powers it."

"Nice," he says admiringly. His large fingers gently run along the wires, tracing them. "Do you use it to power anything else?"

"Yeah, of course," I reply, suddenly bristling at his proximity to my world. His hands are all over it. I'm finding that I kinda like it but then again I really don't. "My iPod, my hair dryer, the fridge, the oven, my cell phone…"

"I get it," he says darkly, straightening up to glare at me. "Take it easy, would you?"

I shake my head. "Whatever. Do you want to clean your arm before it falls off?"

"Are you doing it or am I?"

"You are. I'm not touching it."

I'm not touching you. I think, and the problem is that I actually kind of want to.

He's good looking. Now that I see him in better light, I'm much more aware of that fact. He looks strong, solid. Warm. I haven't been touched by another person in six months and that was old Crazy Crenshaw who lives out in the 'woods' like a wild man by himself. He's helped me a time or two, though both of us made it clear we didn't want each other's company permanently. I went to him when I started running a fever and vomiting awhile back. I couldn't see straight let alone take care of myself. I stumbled to his hideout in an overgrown city park, shambling and moaning like an infected. He took care of me, but when I was better a few days later we went our separate ways. Before that, before he wiped my forehead with a wet cloth and wrapped me up in blankets to fight the chills, I hadn't been touched in four years.

So, yeah, standing in the same room with a guy my age for the first time in my life is throwing me more than a little off balance. As I said, I like it but I don't.

"What's your name?" he asks suddenly.

I blink as I realize we've fallen silent studying each other.

"Jocelyn. Well, Joss," I stammer, my heart racing. I haven't said or heard my own name in a long time. It feels strange on my lips. "What's yours?"

"Ryan."

I immediately think of Jake Ryan in *Sixteen Candles*, my favorite movie. He looks nothing like him but the association is made. This, I understand immediately, will make things so much more complicated.

I turn sharply toward the bathroom. "Let's get you cleaned up. Who knows what germs were in that wolf's mouth? He could have had infected blood in there."

Ryan follows me quickly, understanding the risk he's at. Animals don't contract the virus but they do carry it. If that wolf took down an infected recently, which he very well might have, he could still have active blood in his mouth. The infected don't die, not unless you force them to. The virus doesn't either, making a truly dead zombie almost as dangerous as a mobile one.

I set him up with a couple clean strips of cloth and some alcohol, a tall bottle of Gray Goose vodka I found in a desk in a dentist's office. That and the handful of toothbrushes I scored were the highlight of my week. I hand the bottle to him then quickly leave the room. He can take care of himself, or so I assume since he's still alive. Anyone who couldn't fend for themselves or dress a wound died of starvation or infection years ago.

"So have you always lived here alone?" he calls from my small bathroom. It's a legit bathroom with a toilet and everything that I use leftover washing water to flush once a day. More than that if things are… well you know.

"Yeah," I call back, noticing how my voice echoes over the destroyed hardwood floors up into the vaulted ceilings. I don't usually speak in here. This is already weird. "You in a gang?"

"Yeah. My brother and—hell!" He gags out a curse. I know he just doused his open wound in the alcohol. When he speaks again his voice is a little breathier than before, more strained. "He, uh, he and I joined them when our parents died."

I nod to myself, not surprised. All of us out in the wild are orphans.

"What about you?" he asks, stepping out of the bathroom as he wraps the cloth around his forearm. He's fumbling with it, trying to manage it with one hand. He's failing.

"Here," I hear myself say. I'm across the huge room and standing in front of him before I realize what I'm doing. I wrap the cloth quickly around the wound, being sure to cover it entirely. Nervous, I tie the ends off a little too tightly, pinching him. He doesn't make a sound. "There, that should hold."

"Thanks," he mutters, taking a step back.

I do the same. "Um, yeah, my parents died when I was eight. On Christmas Day."

He winces. "Ouch. Mine went just after Easter."

"When they were talking about a cure?"

"Yeah. They thought it was gonna happen. Kind of let their guard down. Four days after Easter Sunday they were dead and Kevin and I were on our own."

I nod, not sure what to say. *Sorry* is a worthless word.

"The holidays suck," I finally tell him.

He grins. "Yeah, they do."

Chapter Two

The night fully arrives, plunging us in total darkness and letting me breathe a little easier. I prefer the night. More places to hide.

I stand at the giant floor to ceiling windows, looking down on the street below. There's not much to see. Clouds are moving in to cover the moon, which is good because it probably means rain, but it's bad because I can't see a thing. I need to know if the wolves have gone. If the Risen have shown up yet.

"Are they down there?" Ryan asks quietly, his voice close to my ear.

I suppress a jolt of surprise. He sneaks better than I gave him credit for.

"I can't tell yet. You left a lot of blood on the pavement. It's only a matter of time."

"At least the wolves will probably take care of them. They won't stay down there forever."

He's got a point. Once a zombie catches on to human flesh in a location, it's a dog with a bone. It will not give it up. If it were them down there at the gate where the wolves are we would have to count that exit as dead. They'd never leave. If they show up and the wolves are still around, though, there's every chance the animals will kill them and eventually lose interest in us. They'll move on. I have other exits, but that's the safest one. The others involve the roof or windows that offer a jump down to a lower building. It's doable but you risk breaking a bone or tweaking an ankle, two conditions you can't afford out here.

"We'll have to wait it out," I mumble.

I hear him step back. When I look over, he's watching me from a few paces away.

"Are the other rooms here secured?"

I frown, glancing around. "It's a loft... there are no other rooms."

"No, I mean in the building. Have you secured any other rooms besides this one? Any other places where I could crash?"

I look him over sharply. "Is that knife all you have?"

"Yeah. I wasn't thinking. I was—"

"Emotional."

I say it like it's a swear. Like a curse or disease because it is. It's deadly and the longer he's here, the longer I'm in someone else's company, the more likely I am to catch it. I've spent the better part of a decade avoiding that particular plague. I'm not interested in being taken down by it now.

"Yeah, I was. I still am," he admits quietly.

That couldn't have been easy, especially for a Lost Boy. In the wild, your pride and bravado are as important to staying alive as your ability to hunt and avoid being hunted. He's gonna die if he goes back out there. Problem solved for me, no one will know where I live, but if I let that happen then why did I step in in the first place? The logical choice is to let him leave and disappear forever. But now I've seen his face, I've named the puppy and I *emotionally* don't like the idea of him dying.

His disease is catching. It's airborne. It's in his voice. In his eyes.

"You can stay here," I tell him firmly. "In this room. With me. It's fine."

He looks at me in shock, stunned by my offer.

"I don't want to intrude on what you've got here," he says slowly, watching me.

It's a big deal these days to let anyone into your world. I can feel the weight of it in the way my heart is hammering in my chest, my skin prickling with… what? Fear? It must be. It feels like it. This feels like when a Risen is closing in on me, backing me into a corner and threatening to take everything. When Crazy Crenshaw let me stay with him while I was deliriously ill, that was the equivalent of in the old days letting someone wear your underwear or borrow your toothbrush. Inviting someone into your space is incredibly personal. It's basically not done. Letting this guy know where I live is huge enough, but letting him crash here? It's epic. For a recluse like myself it's the apocalypse all over again.

"I said it's fine." I mean to sound sure, solid, but I think I come off angry.

It's because it's not fine. It's terrifying and it's going to be awful, but I can do this. Maybe I need to prove to myself that I can. That I can stay unattached and unemotional. Maybe I want to know I'm a decent human being who can help her fellow man when the chips are down. Or maybe I'm a girl, he's a guy and he's here, a seemingly simple aligning of the stars that has never happened before in my world. One that is unlikely to ever happen again. He's a comet shooting across the sky, his course only bringing him along every hundred years and if I want to experience this once in a lifetime event, I better open my eyes.

"You're sure?" he asks skeptically.

"Do you want me to change my mind?"

"Are any other rooms in this building safe?"

"Nope. Windows are blown out of just about all of them and all of the doors are kicked in."

"Then no, I don't want you to change your mind."

I nod sharply as I turn away, heading deeper into the loft. Away from the window and the darkness outside. Away from him.

"Hey," he calls quietly.

I stop but I don't face him. "What?"

"Thanks. For taking me in tonight and for stepping in with the wolf. I—I made a mistake."

I nod my head slowly, thinking of the mistakes I've seen made. The ones I've made in the past. The ones I'm making now.

"We all do," I say, glancing over my shoulder at him. "Eventually."

I run for the bathroom. I need a minute. I need space in this huge room. A place where I can't see him and I can't feel his eyes. Having someone else around is stranger than I thought it would be. It's harder than I imagined but it's addicting at the same time. I like the sound of his voice as it roams around the room. I like the way he smiles and the fact that despite his idiot move with the wolf he's smart. He's a survivor like me. The problem is my instincts are telling me to get him out of here. Listening for his footsteps, hearing his breathing, sensing his proximity in the room – it's all too much to handle. I'm used to classifying every sound not made by me as a threat. His very existence has me on edge and it's not exactly something I can turn off. I can't tell my brain and body, *hey don't worry about it, he's friendly* and expect them to obey because I trained them for years to worry about everything. To see everyone as a threat. And who knows? Maybe he actually is.

When I get myself pulled together I return to the main area to find him examining the bike again. He's not touching it this time. Just looking.

"How did you learn to do this?" he asks, glancing up at me from his crouched position.

I shrug. "I know a guy."

"You know a guy?" he asks with a grin. "What are you, a mobster? You got connections?"

"Maybe. How do you know about mobsters?"

"I read. How do you know about them?"

"Same. Books. Plus my dad and I used to watch old movies together. He liked old black and whites."

"Do you have any here?"

"No. I don't watch them anymore. I haven't since—you know."

"Yeah, I do. What kind of movies do you have?" he asks, thankfully changing the subject. I don't feel like playing the How Did You Lose Everything game tonight. Or ever.

"Nothing you'd like," I deflect, feeling suddenly embarrassed by my meager collection. All I have is a box set of old 80's movies about kids in high school, something I never got to experience. *Breakfast Club, Fast Times at Ridgemont High, Sixteen Candles, Pretty in Pink.*

"I haven't seen a movie in years. I'll like anything," he insists.

"No, I doubt it."

"What do you have that you're hiding? Are they dirty?"

I frown. "Dirty?"

"Sex tapes. Porn. Skin flicks."

"What?! No!" I exclaim, feeling myself blush for what is probably the first time in my entire life. "They're 80's romantic comedies."

"Cool. Let's watch one. But just for the record, I would have gladly watched a sex tape. No judgment."

"I don't have sex tapes," I grumble.

"No judgment."

"I don't—"

"What's in here now?" he interrupts, kneeling down in front of the small unit.

"Um, *Sixteen Candles*, I think."

I don't think, I know. Images of Jake Ryan dance through my mind as this Ryan invades my home.

"Alright, I'll drive." He hops up on the bike and sits perched ready to go. "How fast do I go? What do I do?"

Apparently this is happening. I'm torn. I feel a little (or a lot) suffocated by his presence. He's so *here*. So actively in the world, in *my* world, it's a little overwhelming for me.

I take a step back.

"I think I, um," I begin, looking anywhere but at him.

"Joss, are you okay?"

My name. Hearing him speak my name is the last straw. It's too much.

"It's going to rain and I need water. I have to go the roof for a bit. I'll be back."

I'm already backing out of the room toward the roof hatch. I can't get out of here fast enough.

"I'll help you."

I hold up my hands to stop him. To ward him off like a dangerous animal. "No, stay. Please stay. I don't want help. Or company."

"Oh." He sits back on the bike slowly, looking surprised.

"Yeah, so stay here. Watch the movie. Just pedal at a regular pace, a steady rhythm you can keep up. I'll be back in a few minutes."

I'm gone for an hour.

I empty the contents of the bucket into a canister I can seal and easily bring downstairs with me, then I position the bucket in the center of the roof just as fat raindrops start to fall. I wish I had more containers here. It rained a couple days ago. I'm sure my rain catchers on the other roofs are doing well, if only I could get to them. I stand outside in the fresh, open air breathing deeply and enjoying the silence but for the rhythm of the rain. It's calming, something I definitely need right now. I listen to the sound of the drops pinging off the bucket, the building, the rest of the world. It fills the gaping, empty spaces left behind by so many dead and if I close my eyes I can pretend they're all still here. Still out there in the rain with their umbrellas and galoshes, hurrying to and from cars carrying groceries, briefcases and babies, going in and out of buildings that aren't decaying or wreaking of rot and ruin.

I drink it in until I can't stand the cold anymore. Until I can't stand my own lies.

When I get back inside I hear the sound of the bike moving. It's sort of surreal, almost a little spooky. Like seeing a ghost. I can also hear the movie, the one I love the most and know by heart. He hasn't noticed me come back in, or else he isn't letting on that he notices, so I sit in the dark as far away from him as I can and I listen.

"When you don't have anything, you don't have anything to lose, right?"

"That's a cheerful thought."

I glance around the dark loft asking myself why I'm courting disaster by having anything that's mine. Anything even vaguely worth defending. Worth fighting for. I also wonder what I'll do with it all now. Now that he knows where I live and I have to leave. Should I try and move it to another building? Should I leave it all behind and start over? I'm exhausted and sad just thinking about it. And angry. At him.

Suddenly Ryan laughs, startling me. The sound fills the large space, drowning out the movie and his pedaling. It reaches me in my far, dark corner, wrapping around me until I feel myself smiling as well. It's stiff, unused for so long, but it's there. For the next half hour I sit on the hard floor with a butt going numb as I listen to Ryan chuckle, laugh and snort at the dialogue. It's a great movie, one about a world we'll never know. Like a fairy tale we've heard a million times about kings, knights and dragons, only this one is about parties and driver's licenses. Things we'll never experience, never see, but want to believe in.

"That's just so my friends won't think, you know, I'm a jerk."

"But they're all pretty much jerks, though, aren't they?"

"Yeah, but the thing is, I'm kinda like the leader, you know? Kinda like the King of the Dipshits."

"How are you not laughing?" Ryan asks,

addressing me but not turning away from the small screen.

"I am," I say, my lie quietly defensive.

"I haven't heard you laugh once."

It's because I don't. I didn't realize it until just now, but I don't laugh, not even at this movie that I love and find so funny. I don't know why. Maybe because it's always been just me and it feels weird to laugh alone. Or maybe I don't find things as funny as I think I do.

"I'm stealthy," I say softly.

He snorts as he glances at me, or at least at the dark corner where I'm sitting.

"You don't like having me here, do you?"

I take a deep breath then let it out slow. "No. Yes. I don't know. I'm not used to it."

"To what?"

"People."

"You've lived alone for a long time?"

"The last six years."

"Whoa," he says, sounding genuinely surprised.

"Yeah."

"Why? Why didn't you join the Colony or a gang?"

I hesitate, hating my answer but knowing it's true. "I got tired of watching people die."

He pedals in silence watching the movie but I don't think he's really paying attention.

"I get that," he finally says, his voice low. I remember that his brother just died. Yeah, he gets it for sure.

"I can't believe I gave my underpants to a geek."

"I heard that," Ryan says.

"Heard what?"

"You chuckled."

I grin in the darkness. He's right.

"Come sit up here," he calls. "You're making me nervous being over there."

I slink out of the shadows. I go as quiet as I can but I know Ryan knows I'm moving. We're both too hyperaware of the world for him not to know. I don't sit close to him. I don't even sit close enough to see the screen because I simply don't need to. By the time the movie is coming to an end I have my eyes closed and I'm mouthing the words silently.

"Thanks for getting my undies back."

"Thanks for coming over."

"Thanks for coming to get me."

"Happy birthday, Samantha. Make a wish."

"It already came true."

Cue the 80's music and the kiss over the cake. Cue the candles and the table and the glowing world inside a warm, happy home. Cue the boy and the girl and the love. Cue the silence and the darkness and the guy on the bike watching me.

Chapter Three

An hour later we hear the groaning. It's a sure sign that his blood on the road has been working like a dinner bell, calling in the dead to chow. We both hurry quietly to the windows to look down. The rain is still falling lightly, something I had hoped would wash away his blood and keep the zombies away. No such luck. Through the very thin amount of light peeking through the clouds we can see a small horde gathering outside. I wait for the wolves to take notice, but they never do. They're already gone.

"They probably left when the rain started," Ryan whispers.

I nod in agreement. "That sucks."

"They know there's blood down there. They'll never leave. Not unless another target comes along."

"We could try to lead them away."

"You mean use ourselves as bait?"

"I was specifically thinking of you as bait, but yes."

"Wouldn't be my first time," he mutters.

I glance at him, but I'm not surprised. I've done it too. We all have, I'm sure.

He meets my eyes and shrugs. "Your home, your

call."

"Do you know this neighborhood?"

"A little," he responds vaguely. "If I had to run I'd make it out. I'm pretty sure."

I nod, thinking. It's tempting. But it's also dangerous. Sure, he could lure the zombies away from my front door and I'd be safe for the night but who's to say they wouldn't lose him and come right back? Obviously the scent of blood and living flesh is strong enough here for them to be swarming. This rain might wash more of it away but how soon?

"What would your gang do?"

"We'd kill them. We always kill them when we can."

"Do you think we can?"

He shakes his head. "I don't know. I can't count them. Maybe."

"You willing to work with a maybe?"

He grins. "A maybe, one knife and a busted hand? How could it go wrong?"

"We can do something about the knife."

"I almost want to stick with it just to see if I can do it."

"Yeah, well," I begin, leading him toward the wall beside the door, "I'd rather you didn't try to get me killed again."

There's a large, discolored drop cloth hanging from the wall. I pull it aside to unveiling my collection. Ryan's eyes light up as he whistles at the sight.

"Joss, I'm gonna be honest with you." He reverently runs his hand over each tool, all of them dented, dinged, mangled and well used. Well worn. Well wielded. "If you weren't so hostile, I'd be in love with you by now."

I can't understand that statement and I can't look him in the eyes, so I stick to what I know. Silence.

He picks up a weapon; a tire iron. Not your average, store it in the trunk of your car tire iron. This one is long and incredibly sharp at one end, round and blunt on the other.

"That's really not the best—" I begin, but he cuts me off with a smile.

"It's perfect." He swings it around, spinning it back and forth, testing its weight and reach.

I grab my go to weapon, the most used of them all.

"Is that what I think it is?"

In answer I whip my hand out. The baton extends to its full length of 16 inches. It's all steel, all deadly.

"It's an ASP," I reply proudly.

"That is killer."

I can't stop the chuckle from rising out of my chest. I flip it in my hand, offering the handle to him. He takes it up eagerly to test it out with a couple practice swings.

"It can break bone, can't it?"

"Oh yeah," I say with a nod. "It'll crack skulls."

"Where did you get this and are there more of them?" He collapses it down then swings it out as I did, snapping the baton out to attention. He laughs when it extends.

"I found it in an apartment years ago. It was the only one."

"Dammit."

"I know. I did a happy dance when I found it."

He hands it back to me. "You happy dancing? I can't picture it."

"I'd rather you didn't."

"I'd rather see it."

"That's not going to happen." I stash the ASP in my pocket and lift the wood from the door. "You ready for this?"

"I'm always ready."

I look back at him, eyebrows raised. "How's your hand?"

He rolls his eyes at me. I hate the gesture so much I feel a little like punching him again. "I told you, I made a mistake. It was one time."

"Your one time mistake almost got both of us killed. It still might."

"I said I was sorry."

"No," I say, shaking my head, "you did not. When did this imaginary apology happen?"

"Well I meant to say it."

I lean back against the unsecured door, crossing my arms over my chest.

"What?" he asks impatiently.

"I'm waiting."

"Seriously?" When I don't respond he sighs heavily. "Joss, I am so terribly sorry. Please forgive me."

His voice is dead, completely insincere. I continue to wait.

He sighs again as his shoulders slump slightly. "I'm sorry."

"Thank you," I say happily, popping up off the door and swinging it open.

Before I head out into the hall I look both ways like I'm crossing the street. I've been blindsided by a zombie before. It's like being hit by a truck that's all teeth, drool and stink. It sticks with you.

"Is this really a good idea?" he whispers as we step out into the hall.

"Now?" I whisper back sharply. "You're asking that question now?"

"I'm just saying maybe we should wait until first light."

I know what he's really worried about; squaring off with Risen with an untested partner. Fighting with the wrong person, or another person at all, can prove fatal. You put your faith in them to cover you in some way but what if they make a mistake? What if they fail you? What do you do then?

You let the infected have them and you run, that's what.

Then you live alone and you keep your mouth and memory shut.

I shake my head, not willing to let him use this lame excuse. It's a shady way of saying I don't trust you.

"You know why that's stupid."

"Because there will be more of them by then," he mutters grudgingly.

"Exactly. If we kill what's out there now, they'll work as a deterrent for others. They don't come around their own stink."

"We're gonna have to clear them though."

"No we won't."

"What? Now who's being stupid? You have to clear them or people will know you live around here. Dead undead on your doorstep is like a Welcome mat to Colonists. Your home could be compromised."

"It already is," I say, my quiet voice dripping with venom.

He touches my arm, stopping me. I make a point of looking up at his eyes and ignoring where he's touching me even though the contact is searing my skin through my clothes. He does it like it's nothing and I think to him, having lived with his brother and surrounded by other people, it's just that; nothing. They probably touch each other all the time. To me, though, it's everything and it's almost as beautiful as it is frightening.

"You're talking about me?" he whispers, his brow furrowing.

"Of course I'm talking about you. You know where I live. You know what I have. I can't stay here anymore. When you leave tomorrow morning, so will I."

"For good?" I nod and he shakes his head, clearly annoyed. "You don't have to do that. I swear to you, I'm not a threat."

"Maybe not now because you don't need anything. But what happens in a month or so when the winter hits hard? What if you need something you know I have? What if your gang loses control of their home and it's cold outside and you're desperate? You're swearing to me that you won't lead them all straight to me?"

"Yes," he says, his eyes hard.

I shake my head. "I don't know you. Your word means nothing to me."

His jaw clenches as his hand tightens on my arm. He's angry.

"I hate the thought of you losing your home because you saved me."

I roughly shake off his hand. "You and me both."

When we get to the gate at the bottom of the stairs I miss the wolves. If they were still here the dead wouldn't be. The wolves would have made quick work of them, shredding them to pieces and leaving nothing but a disgusting, comforting pile of gore and guts. The animals don't eat the zombies. In fact, most of them stay clear of them, predators being the only ones who attack them. You can tell they're around when deer go blazing by you down an alley or in the middle of a mall. Birds will take to the skies screaming and screeching like crazy. They're a natural warning system but even they can fail you. Even the wolves will let you down sometimes.

Waiting at the gate for us is a group of eight dead. Eight bobbing heads. Eight gaping, moaning mouths that I can smell from here, the thick rot of their insides wafting up and out toward us with each movement. Eight sets of hands clawing through the gate, some clawing through each other not caring if it hurts or if it's right.

It's a lot of them. More than I've seen rounded up in one spot lately. They're disappearing slowly, either being picked off by aggressive animals or by us, the remaining vigilante humans living in the wild. The people in the Colonies should be thanking us, maybe throwing a little of that homemade bread our way now and then for the service we're performing. One day the outside world will once again be zombie free and they'll have us to thank for it. The ones who refused to hide behind their walls and tend their fields. The ones still fighting the good fight. People like Ryan and I.

"How do you wanna do this?" he asks. "Kill who we can through the gate? Open it up and try to shove them back into the street? Let them start coming up the stairs and pick 'em off one, maybe two at a time?"

"If we had a gun, I'd say kill 'em through the gate."

"But we don't."

I shake my head sharply. "Nope, we don't. So that's out. I don't like the idea of getting out in the open with them where they can surround us."

"Right, going into the street is sketchy. We'd also have to push them back which means close contact in close quarters." He looks at me with a grimace. "I sort of hate that."

"Me too," I agree heartily. "But opening the gate and letting them come at us means close quarters too and we both have melee weapons. Can't really get a good swing in this stairwell. Especially not side by side. We might accidentally hit each other."

He smirks. "Tell me how much that idea bothers you."

"At the moment, you're more inconvenient to me unconscious or dead than alive."

"I'm glad you're warming up to me."

I snort derisively.

"So…" he says slowly. "What do you want to do?"

I sigh as I rub my hand over my eyes, feeling tired. "Go back upstairs, eat dinner and watch another movie."

Beside me I feel his chuckle as much as I hear it. We're pressed in tight together standing in front of this door with sixteen pair, wait, no an odd fifteen (someone's missing one) opaque eyes staring at us.

"What are we having for dinner?" Ryan asks.

"Homemade waffles, hot off the skillet."

"With fresh strawberries?"

"And whipped cream."

"Scrambled eggs."

"And bacon."

"*Lots* of bacon," he says emphatically.

My mouth is watering. I regret playing this game. My cold carrots and potatoes are going to taste especially bland now.

"Let's get this over with." I glance at him questioningly. "Shove them back? Get the range to beat their heads in?"

He nods once. "Sounds good. On my count?"

"Go."

"Three… two… one!"

I unlatch the gate and we kick it out toward them. It connects with the two that were pressed against it and shoves them back into the throng. They all jostle loosely, one falling down completely. I'd rather he'd stayed vertical because now we've got a potential ankle biter to worry about.

"Crawler on my side!" I shout to Ryan in warning. "Watch the floor."

"Got it! I'll cover you while you take him out."

As we push the horde back, avoiding snapping jaws and clawing fingers as best we can, I keep an eye on the floor. The group tramples over their fallen buddy, reluctantly giving up ground to us as we push them back with weapons held out against their chests. I have to let my mind go blank as we get this close to them, as we intentionally touch them. I can feel the texture of their skin beneath the remnants of their clothes. It's waxy and disturbing in its cold malleability. I worry my fingers or knuckles are going to sink into their flesh, tearing through the skin and driving right down to the bone. And they wouldn't even flinch.

They're hideous and strong, stronger than you would believe, but they're also clumsy as hell. They push back against us hard but all it takes is a swift kick to the knee and they stumble, making it easier to push them. You just have to be careful not to get overzealous or you end up with more crawlers.

I have nightmares about crawlers.

When this one's head is in sight and the horde is almost out the second doorway and into the street, I step quickly to the side, leaving Ryan exposed on his left. I don't like doing it, to him or myself, but this guy on the floor has got to go. I lift the ASP and line up the shot like a golfer. When I swing the steel ball at the end toward his temple I know it'll do its job. People I can't count on but steel is a faithful friend. The resounding *crack!* that echoes through the entryway and reverberates all the way up my arms tells me this Risen is no more.

I quickly fall in line beside Ryan again to help him push the remainders outside. Once we're clear of the doorway we spread out slightly to give each other room but we keep our backs to the wall. You learn that real quick, alone or with an army. Keep your back defended.

The dead heavily favor Ryan, probably drawn in by his injured hand and the blood readily available at the surface of his skin. Five of them move to surround him while only two stick with me.

"Hell," I mutter, not liking his odds.

It shouldn't bother me, but it does. I shouldn't care if he makes it or not, but I do.

For the second time today I play the reluctant hero.

I step away from the wall and take a huge swing at the zombie closest to me. He goes down quickly, the side of his face soundly bashed in and turned quickly to gray mush. I ignore the other one who's on me and I hurry to Ryan. My back is exposed making me feel naked in the cold night air, rain falling over me, matting my hair to my face. I take a quick, hard swing at the kneecap on one of Ryan's zombies. It drops to the ground, unable to hold its weight on the badly broken leg. They don't feel pain but a broken leg is still a problem for them. It's like chopping off a hand. Whether they feel it or not, that limb is now useless.

I do the same to another zombie, a young boy, only this time I take out his leg at the shin. The bone pops out through his skin, spraying his black tar blood over the sidewalk. He topples over. I want to say it bothers me brutalizing a child but it doesn't. Live in this world long enough and the dead are just that – dead. It doesn't walk like a child or talk like a child so it's pretty easy to accept that it's no longer a child. Moral qualms put to rest. If you're uncomfortable with that, go join the Colonies.

"Joss, your six!" Ryan calls out as he stabs the sharp end of the iron straight into a Risen's eye. It slides in smoothly and the zombie crumples, slipping slowly off the steel.

"I know," I growl.

I'm aware of it, have been the whole time. It's about three paces behind me and closing. I spin quickly, bringing up the ASP and making contact on its face. I make sure to close my eyes and mouth when I hit it because sometimes you get exploders. Like a rotten pumpkin that blows up when you toss it against the pavement or kick it in. Dead and dusty as it may look, sometimes it retains some of its juices. This one sure does. I feel the spray hit me in the face and I immediately use the inside of my coat to wipe it clear. I'm not worried about infection, not really. Mostly it's just gross.

When I turn around, Ryan has taken out the crawlers I created and is working on the last of the standing. He rears back then slams the sharp end of the tire iron into the Risen's mouth. It crunches when it hits bone in the back of the skull. Ryan immediately jerks down hard on his end, letting out an angry shout. It pries the zombies jaw off the hinges and I'm pretty sure it snaps the spinal cord. Either way, the dead get deader.

"You okay?" Ryan asks, breathing heavy.

His hair is soaked by the rain like mine and he runs his hand through it, spiking it up off his forehead. His eyes are big and excited from the adrenaline of the kill. I imagine that despite my bad attitude I probably look about the same. You never learn to like it, this life, but eventually you do learn to enjoy the highs. Being outnumbered by Risen and coming out unscathed, that's a high. A big one.

"Yeah, I'm great," I say, almost meaning it.

He glances around at our handiwork. "Let's pull them into the building, stow them in an empty room."

"Why bother?"

"Because that way no one will see them, not unless they're already in the building. The rain will wash away most of this." He gestures to the pooling black mess pouring out of the zombies onto the pavement.

"I'm leaving anyway."

"But this could buy you some time. You don't have to leave so soon."

"I have to leave when you leave."

He shakes his head as he runs his hand over his hair again, clearly frustrated. "Let's just do this, let's take care of this problem and we can sort any others out later."

"Fine, okay," I agree, stowing my ASP and pushing my wet mass of hair out of my face. "Let's pull them inside and get out of this rain. As much as I want a shower, I'm getting cold."

Chapter Four

"You're not in a gang but you're trading with someone," Ryan comments, munching on a carrot.

We're working through a bag of vegetables I've pulled out that I got from Crazy Crenshaw in exchange for meat. He's not a hunter, not even close. He's a gardener. Of all kinds of things. All kinds of plants, if you get my meaning. He's always trying to trade me certain herbs for the meat I bring him but I stick to veggies. Ryan was surprised at how large the vegetables are. Apparently Lost Boys are poor gardeners as well and I wonder if it's not a skill possessed solely by the older generation.

"Why do you say that?" I ask, averting his eyes.

I don't want to talk about Crenshaw. He trades with Lost Boys but I don't know which ones exactly. I'm not about to go talking about him to someone he might want to avoid.

He waves his carrot at me, getting my attention. "No way you grew this somewhere in here. Not unless you have a garden on the roof?"

I shake my head. "There's nothing on this roof."

"I didn't think so."

"So what are you getting at?"

He takes a bite of the carrot. "Nothing. Just making an observation."

"It feels more like an invasion."

"Or a conversation," he says with a grin.

I roll my eyes and take a sip of water from my canister, washing down the dry, cold broccoli I've been working on. And it is work. Unfulfilling yet nourishing work.

"Does your gang trade in the markets?" I ask, changing the subject while offering him the canister.

He takes a sip from it as well, his mouth on the cool metal almost exactly where mine was. I blush yet again. I'm setting a record or making up for lost time. It's embarrassing either way. I don't like things I can't control.

"You've been to the markets?" he asks, sounding surprised.

I shake my head firmly, chuckling slightly at the idea of me showing up there. "No, never. But I've seen them happening. They're hard to miss."

"Seeing all of us rounded up like that, it must be your worst nightmare."

"Crawlers."

"What about crawlers?"

"Crawlers are my worst nightmare."

He nods his head. "That's a legitimate fear."

"What's yours?"

"What's my worst fear?"

"Yeah. You know mine. Now you owe me yours."

He laughs as he leans back on his palms, looking relaxed. "No way."

"It's part of the deal. Spill it."

"I made no such deal. You really haven't been to the markets. You would know that you don't give up anything without knowing exactly what you're going to get in return." He grins at me crookedly. "And you're gettin' nothin'.'"

I shake my head in disgust. "I hate people."

"I hear ya."

I study him for a moment, unsure if I want to tread on sacred ground. In the end curiosity wins out over etiquette.

"Do you like the people in your gang?" I ask quietly.

He stares at me for a long time and I worry I shouldn't have asked. It's a delicate thing to talk about. I don't want to know the name of his gang or their location, basically any identifying information whatsoever. He owes it to his crew to keep them and their location a secret. Also, it's important to me that he never think of me as a liability. As a mouth that needs silencing. I'm just about to tell him to forget it when he shrugs.

"I guess. Not all of them all of the time, but for the most part, yeah. I wouldn't stick with them if I didn't like them." He sits forward again and studies the pattern on the now empty veggie bag. It has a pink Hello Kitty on it. Don't judge, I have my reasons for keeping it. "I think I stayed with them for as long as I did because of my brother. He likes... liked this group of guys. I got offers to join larger gangs. To live bigger and better, but I always stayed because of Kev."

I don't want to talk about his brother. I know that sounds calloused and that's because I am; I'm calloused. I have a hard exterior and none of the soft, nougaty center to balance it out. I've worked hard to sink the callouses down deep, layer after layer until I'm more Jawbreaker than anything else.

"Was it The Hive?"

He looks at me silently with guarded eyes.

"I only ask because you said 'live bigger and better' and from what I've seen, no one but the Colonies lives bigger and better than The Hive," I explain. "I'm not... I know you're not one of them because of your neck. I don't want to know what gang you're in."

He lifts his hand to touch the clean skin of his neck. If he were a member of The Hive, the largest gang in the area shamelessly living completely unhidden in the aquarium down at the wharf, he would have a hornet tattooed there. The Hive is huge by normal standards, easily 70 people strong. Probably more. Everyone knows where they are but no one would dare attack them. Not even the Colonies, it seems. There are two in the CenturyLink and Safeco stadiums just a couple miles from the aquarium but as far as I know they've never clashed with The Hive. I find that both amazing and suspicious.

"You're not even a little curious?"

I look at him hard. "Don't tell me."

"I wasn't going to," he says, chuckling. "I was only asking if you were curious."

"I'm not."

"Okay."

A silence falls between us and I struggle for something to talk about. Hunting? No. Animal pelts? No. Jerky crafting? Ugh, no. Chit chat is not my strong suit.

"How'd you end up alone like this?" he eventually asks.

"I don't want to talk about it."

He nods in understanding. "Alright. How about

this? What's your worst memory of the early days?"

I scowl at him. "You mean aside from everybody dying?"

He waves the question away. "Everybody's messed up from that. What else have you got? What's on your apocalypse highlight reel?"

"This is a really dark question."

"You strike me as a really dark girl."

I hesitate. Am I flattered by that? No, that makes no sense. Still, though....

"You tell me yours first."

"Nope, not a chance," he says with a shake of his head. "But we'll make a deal. Marketplace 101. If you tell me your most messed up moment from the beginning, I'll tell you mine."

I think about my answer but I try not to go too deep. I don't want to dig too far and pull out something truly ugly. A lot of this stuff from the early days is buried and gone as far as I'm concerned and I'm not about to go grave robbing to entertain him.

"I wore boy's clothes for the first year."

"That's it?" he asks me, sounding annoyed. "That's your worst?"

"No, not by a long shot, but you asked what was on my highlight reel and that is. I had to wear boy's clothes for the first year because the people who took me in were afraid to travel with a young girl. They hacked my hair off and made me wear baseball hats and Teenage Mutant Ninja Turtle shirts."

"You should have been wearing those anyway. They were awesome."

"I'm not arguing that. Now what's yours?"

He chuckles. "You think you get my worst in trade for that?"

"No, but I get something off your list. Something scarring." I point my finger at his face. "Your rules, remember?"

"Alright, alright," he laughs, surrendering. He thinks for a bit before saying, "We made the mistake of going to the zoo a couple months after it happened. My parents wanted to look for food, bottled water, a place to hide. They figured with it being fenced in that maybe the virus hadn't had much room to spread there, if at all."

"Had it?"

"Nah, it was pretty empty. There were a few employees and tourist types that were taken down by it. They were wandering around looking confused and hungry by then. The other inhabitants, though, that's why we had to leave. That's what was messed up. Kev and I couldn't handle that nightmare."

"What nigh— Oh no, those poor animals!"

"Yeah. Every last one of them starved in their cage. Some had eaten others and it wasn't always the animal you'd think that was left last." He shivers quickly and shakes it off. "Can you imagine what the prisons were like?"

"Maybe they let the prisoners out."

"I doubt it."

"I'm not so sure about that," I mutter.

"Why do you say that?"

"Because it seems like most of the people out there belong in prison."

He nods in agreement. "You're right. But that's just the way things are, I think. Kill or be killed kind of thing. You get so used to fighting and killing the zombies, maybe it doesn't seem so crazy to kill other people anymore. At least to survive."

"Is that how you feel?"

He shrugs, looking away. "No. Maybe. I'm not gonna go out looking for people to kill, but if someone busted in here and threatened me or yo—yeah, if I feel threatened enough, I'll kill another person."

I pause, unsure if I should ask the next question. I don't know if he'll answer and I don't know if I want him to. But messed up as I am, I'm not a coward.

"Have you?"

He meets my eyes, challenging me with them. "Have I what?"

"Have you killed another person?"

"Yeah. I have," he replies bluntly, his eyes unflinching.

"I haven't."

"I know."

I scowl at him. "How do you know?"

"Because you're looking at me like I'm dangerous. Like I'm questionable. If you'd done it too, if you knew what it was like to be backed that hard against a wall, you wouldn't be judging me now."

"I'm not judging you."

"Yes you are. And it's okay. I'm not proud of it, not like the psychopaths out there that do it for fun. But I'm not sorry either."

There's a long silence that I have no idea how to fill. I look anywhere but at him, unsure where we go from here. After this, what is there to talk about?

"Don't be scared of me," he says quietly.

My eyes shoot to his, surprised. He's looking at me with steel in his gaze but there's something else there too. Something almost sad.

"I'm not."

He nods once. "Good."

"Does it bother you that you've—"

"Can we go outside?" he asks, standing up suddenly. "The rain has stopped. Maybe we could hit the roof? I'm feeling closed in here."

I look around the massive room we're sitting in with its twelve foot ceilings and nearly total lack of walls and I wonder what he's talking about. But I don't ask. When we head for the door I pause for a moment, debating, then hold up a finger to him.

"Wait."

I dig around in my backpack, searching. What I need is so small it fits in my two coat pockets, making it easy to hide it from him.

"Okay. Let's go," I say, hurrying up through the hatch.

When we get to the roof I immediately check the rain bucket. I'm relieved to find it far fuller than it was before. Water is my worry, far bigger than my concern for food.

"You're good?" Ryan asks, watching me smile at my bucket.

"For a bit, yeah. I still need to go get more tomorrow."

"I won't drink anymore."

"Don't be stupid. Of course you can drink some."

"I don't want to make you go out to the watering holes if you don't have to. They're dangerous lately."

I haven't told him I have other water sources. That I don't go to the holes. Ever. They're communal type areas where water pools (old fountains, swimming pools, etc.) where people go to gather rain water. They're dangerous no matter what, but for someone like me living alone and fending for herself, they're a nightmare. A death sentence.

"Have you seen a lot of Risen there?"

"No. We don't go there very often. We do what you do – capture the rain – but on a much larger scale. But we've heard things from other gangs. Stuff about what's been going on at the holes."

"What's happening?"

"Roundups. A lot of them."

The Colonies. They perform roundups of the survivors in the wild, a lot like a dogcatcher picking up strays. It's not voluntary. Not anymore. If they find you, especially if you're young, they'll take you by force back to one of the compounds and keep you there. It used to be they rumbled around town in their trucks and called out over loudspeakers for people looking for sanctuary to join them. They offered a warm, dry bed, larger meals than a lot of us could remember ever eating and safety from the infected. All you had to do was follow them like the Pied Piper out to their compound where you'd work to pay your way.

Now, though, it isn't so merry. Now they scour the city in run down vehicles that run silently, electric most likely, and snatch people off the streets. They write messages on old billboards and on the sides of buildings trying to drum up new recruits.

Be part of a community again! Serve a purpose!

We have doctors! Nurses! Teachers! Farmers! All we need is YOU!

They promise everything under the sun to get us to join willingly. They single out young people, advertising working generators and game systems on large TVs. Hot showers. Hot meals. Milk! That right there, even on my strongest of days, could almost persuade me to go along with them. But I never do. Something just isn't right about it. They act like they're trying to save us, saying we are lost and they would return us to the fold where we'd be safe and sound, but I don't know these people. Not one of them. How can I be returned to somewhere I've never been?

"What do you have in your pockets?"

"What?" I ask, blinking at him. I hadn't realized I'd zoned out.

It's getting really late. I'm getting tired and I need to sleep. But I know I won't. I can't. The comet is still shooting across the sky and I don't want to miss it.

"You pulled something out of your bag before coming up here," Ryan says, gesturing to my pockets. "What was it?"

I smile with excitement and step closer to him, eager to show him. If he thought the TV was cool...

"Is that—does it work?" he asks, staring at my open hands.

"Yeah, it does. I wasn't kidding before. I use the bike to charge it."

"I thought you were being a smart ass."

"Well, I was," I admit, carefully plugging a short black cord into the top of the iPod in my hand. "I don't have a hairdryer or a cell phone."

"Or a fridge or oven?"

"Nope, sorry."

"Don't be sorry, just turn it on," he says excitedly. His eyes are bright with anticipation. "I haven't heard music in... God, in forever."

"You guys don't have any power?"

"Not really. Just some broke down solar panels that hardly work anymore. And no one has stuff like this," he says, pointing to the device as the screen lights up. It makes our faces glow a bluish-white in the near perfect darkness. I worry for a moment, thinking it's like lighting the Bat Signal up here. If anyone is watching the skyline they'll notice. They'll know we're here.

"Here," Ryan says, stepping close to me and wrapping his arms around me lightly. The iPod is pressed between us, the light of the small screen now mostly trapped. "Better?"

"Better," I mumble, keeping my head down over the screen as I scroll through it. I can feel his heat coming up out of the neck of his jacket. His chin and cheek are brushing against my temple and his breath is in my hair, warm and ticklish.

"Do you have batteries in the speakers?" His voice rumbles right beside my ear.

I shake my head slightly. I hook the speakers to the belt loop on my jeans. "No. They don't need power. They're not very good, but—"

"But it's better than nothing."

"I think so."

I pick a song to play for him. My favorite, because why not share them all with him tonight? Why not let the things I love out to breath and exist for eyes and ears other than my own? I'm finding that it makes them fresh and new to me again. Brighter and shinier than they've ever been. Myself included.

I dare to glance up at him and see his eyes are closed. I look down again quickly, feeling like an intruder on something sacred.

"Do you like it?" I whisper to him.

"I love it."

I smile. It's getting easier.

When the song comes to an end I feel Ryan take a deep breath. I look up at him again to see he's smiling. His eyes are shining in the darkness.

"It's so… full," he whispers. "I've heard people play guitar or sing, but not like that. Not so many voices and instruments all at once. Not in a long, long time." He chuckles at himself and closes his eyes again. "Can we listen to it one more time?"

When the music begins again his arms tighten around me, pulling me closer. We're not hiding the iPod anymore. It's flattened between us, our bodies pressed together from head to toe, only my arms folded up between us keeping us apart. He's holding me to him and I have to fight the overpowering urge to rest my head on his shoulder. To free my arms and wrap them around him as well. I'm at the tip of the arc, at the closest point where the comet travels by the earth. I want to reach out my hand and trail my fingers through its shimmering tail of gray dust and starlight. I want a piece of it to stay with me, to cling to me and be one more thing I carry with me forever. One more load I happily bear.

But I don't because it's all an illusion. The star that looks so close, close enough to touch, is really millions of miles away. It's only passing through. It's lighting up my night and my life for one brief shining moment, then it will be gone and I'll have to forever make due with the memory. And that's okay. That's what's safe. What's smart.

When the song ends I pull away with a wan smile. Ryan looks at me over the light of the iPod glowing like a candle between us. He leans toward me, only slightly. My heart hammers in my chest.

If you don't have anything, you don't have anything to lose.

The light blinks out.

I step away, making him frown.

The arc is ending. The comet starts its return to space.

Chapter Five

"Are you asleep?"

"Yes."

"Are you lying?" he asks with a chuckle.

"No. I talk in my sleep."

There's silence. I think he's given up and gone to sleep, but then there's his voice filling the empty room again, making it feel small.

"Why do you live alone, Joss?"

I close my eyes and breathe deeply through my nose. I wish he'd stop saying my name. No one says my name anymore, not even Crazy Crenshaw. It's foreign and familiar. It's soothing and it hurts like hell.

"I told you why," I answer warily. "I got sick of watching people die."

"Not everybody dies."

I can't help but laugh at how absurdly wrong that statement is. "Yes they do."

"Okay, yes, *eventually* everyone dies. But you know what I mean. Not everyone is going to die that way."

"And what way is that?"

"Violently."

"Everyone I know who has died, died that way."

I hear him sigh heavily then shift under his blankets. I can feel his eyes on me.

"You shouldn't be alone."

"Says who?" I ask sharply.

"Says logic," he replies just as sharply. "No one should be alone like this."

"It's been working for the last six years. Don't try to fix what's not broken."

"I'm not saying you're broken, I'm just saying I wish you weren't alone."

"I wish a lot of things, Ryan." My voice is growing hard, hot. "I wish my parents hadn't died. I wish zombies didn't exist. I wish I could have ice cream. But most of all, more than any of that, I wish you'd never shown up outside my building."

Because then I wouldn't remember what being alone really is.

"I wish that too," he agrees quietly. "Now I have to go back and know you're out here alone."

"I won't be here. Tomorrow I will be so far away from here."

"Where are you going to go?"

I laugh again, brittle and angry. "I'm not telling you that. That's the point of leaving. So you can't ever find me again."

"Are you being a jerk right now so I won't want to?"

I turn my head and glare at him. He watches me passively and it pisses me off more than anything else.

"I'm being a jerk because that's what I am. I don't play well with others, okay? I don't want other people in my life just so they can disappear. I'm tired of finding things just so I can lose them. Like my home and everything in it. I'm losing all of that tomorrow because of you, do you get that? You've cost me everything. My home, my safety. And all for what? Revenge you didn't even get. Against an animal!"

He looks at me with his large brown eyes and I see the regret in them. The sadness. The pity.

"I'm sorry," he says earnestly. "You have no idea how sorry I am."

Tears sting my eyes. I can't stand it. I leap up, grabbing my sleeping bag.

"You already said that. It didn't change anything then and it certainly doesn't change anything now. I'm going to the roof to get some sleep and in the morning when I come back down I expect you to be gone. Take what you want with you, I can't carry all of it out and it will save you and your boys some trouble later when you loot the place."

I turn to leave. I hear him hurriedly stand up behind me.

"Joss, wait."

"Stop saying my name!" I cry, my voice cracking.

I hate myself for it. For being weak, for being cruel, for being so, so, so angry. Angrier than I ever realized I was but with him here now I can feel it. I can nearly taste it. I take a deep shuddering breath, willing the tears back. I haven't cried in years and I can't start now. I'll be like an addict taking a hit of heroine for the first time in a decade. I'll never be able to stop.

When I speak, I will my voice to be even and calm. "Just go, please. It's almost dawn. You'll be alright. Take a weapon with you. Or two or five, whatever. Take anything, but please just go."

"I'll go," he answers, his voice deep and low. "I'm leaving."

I nod. "Good. That's good."

"Just promise me something. One thing."

"What?"

"Don't leave. Please trust me when I tell you that I won't ever tell anyone you're here. I'll never tell anyone about you at all. Just don't go. I can't stand the thought of you having to start over."

I don't respond. I don't have words, not any which are true. So I duck my head down, feel the angry heat of a single tear on my cheek and I climb the stairs to the roof.

I don't sleep. I also don't hear him leave but I know he's gone. He's quiet as a mouse, quieter even than me, and it's no surprise that he could slip out without being heard. My world slips back into place, back into the gray numb of pure survival that it's been in for the last however many years. Maybe all of them. Maybe since Christmas and my Cabbage Patch Doll. Since the end of everything.

When dawn comes I creep back into the loft but it's not my home anymore. Mentally I've already moved out. I'm trying to decide where I'm going to go, which part of town I should try to find shelter in or if I should cut my loses and finally take the plunge and move into the woods. That's when I see the writing on the wall.

7th/Boren
red brick
I know urs, u know mine
don't go

"Oh my God," I breathe, my hand against my mouth.

He's given me his address. It's his toothbrush, his underwear, the key to his diary all wrapped up into one. If his crew knew about this they would beat him down and throw him out on the streets. This is a dangerous thing he's done. I search the room, looking for a rag to wipe it clean with. I can't leave it here. Anyone who finds it will know right where they live. I can't believe he left this!

I see the red brick lying on the ground beside the gray cement wall. This is what he wrote it with. He used the edge like chalk. I grab the brick and prepare to scrape the words out, to draw over them until they are unrecognizable. But I freeze, my hand holding the stone hovering over his writing.

I know urs, u know mine

He gave up all he could to try and make us square. To try and make me stay.

I look around the room to do a quick inventory. It's all here. Everything. Even the tire iron he used to fight with last night. He didn't take anything to help him get home and that realization makes my gut clench with guilt. I'm worried he might not have made it home last night. I'm sure he left immediately after I asked him to which means he left in the dark. In an unfamiliar neighborhood. With only a knife and a huge gaping wound on his hand.

"Son of a—"

I drop the brick and grab my coat, throwing it on as I pocket my ASP and sheath my knife on my hip. I quickly whip open the door and blindly run into the hall.

I should have looked both ways.

I immediately trip and fall flat on my face.

"Owwww," I groan, clutching my elbow.

"Are you alright?" Ryan asks, reaching out for me.

I roll away from him onto my back and clutch my arm to me, riding out the crazy weird tingles and shocks passing through it.

"I hit my funny bone and it wasn't funny," I moan. I kick my foot at him and catch him in the hip.

"Ah, what!?" he cries, scooting away. He grabs hold of my foot as it comes back for more.

"You tripped me! Can you even function without screwing with my life?"

"Actually, you stepped on me and fell. I'm more the victim here than you are."

I kick vainly at him again. "Why are you lying on the floor in my hallway?"

"Because I couldn't lock the door."

I lift my head up and stare at him. "What?"

"Your door, it only locks from the inside. I went to leave and realized I'd be leaving you defenseless but you wanted me gone so I camped out here. I was going to go once I heard you moving around inside, but I fell asleep." He picks up a chunk of rotted out carpet and chucks it at me. "Then you stepped on me and started kicking me. So, you know, you're welcome."

I sit up, still cradling my angry arm. "Is that really your address? That's where your gang lives."

"No, I lied for the hell of it. Yes, it's where we live."

"Why would you do that?" I ask incredulously. "That is so dangerous to put that out there like that. And not just for you, for all of them."

"I know. That's why I told you. I knew you'd understand."

"Understand what? That you can't be trusted?"

He frowns. "Wait, what?"

"They trust you to keep that information on lock and you go writing it on walls in random rooms across town? You knowing where I live, that's one thing. But putting it out for the world where your entire crew lives, that's crazy. And reckless. And so stupid."

"You're missing the point. We're square. Now you don't have to move."

"No, I still have to move. But thanks, now I know what part of town to stay away from."

"No, you don't move. That's why—How are you not getting this?!"

"Oh, I get it. You make terrible decisions. That's what I'm getting."

He pauses then puts his hand up, silencing me. "Hold up. Where were you going in such a hurry?"

"What?"

"You. You came slamming out of the apartment without even glancing in the hall or you would have seen me laying here. Where were you going in such a hurry?"

I don't answer but I don't look away either. I hold his stare, keeping my face impassive.

He grins. "You were going after me, weren't you?"

"I was coming to look for your corpse."

His grin becomes a smile. "You were worried about me."

"No. Kind of. You didn't arm yourself before you left and I didn't want that on my head so, yes, I was going to look for you to make sure you were alright."

"That's nice of you."

I roll my eyes and look down the long ugly

hallway. Anywhere but at him.

"I'm not a complete jerk," I mumble.

"I shouldn't have said that."

"Well, you did."

"I know and I wish I hadn't."

I shake my head. "We need to stop wishing for things."

"How 'bout we start doing things instead." He stands and offers me his hand. "Walk with me. I'll show you where I live."

Chapter Six

The rain has left the world looking shiny and bright. When we hit the sidewalk outside my building I'm pleasantly surprised to find no evidence of the zombies we killed out here last night. Since no more showed up later on I'm assuming the rain took care of Ryan's blood too. Everything is as it should be, aside from the eight corpses now rotting in a nearby room inside. But that actually works to my advantage. They'll mask my scent and keep zombies and animals both away. Animals don't like the dead when they're walking and they certainly don't like them when they're rotting for the last time. If it weren't for Ryan knowing about me I could stay here.

I'm not crazy and I'm not so stubborn that I can't entertain the idea that he's on the up and up. He may very well be able to keep me a secret no matter what happens with him and his crew. But it's a big question mark and one too dangerous to gamble on. I want to stay, I really do, and honestly I want to trust him. But I don't. I can't.

"You should get a rain system started," he whispers, poking his head around a building to scan the road.

"I've got one."

"The bucket?"

I shrug. "Among other things."

"In other places?" he asks, looking at me sideways. I return his stare but I don't answer. Eventually he nods. "It's smart. It's better than going to the holes."

"I never go to the holes."

"Good."

I frown at him. "Why do you care?"

He chuckles as he shakes his head.

"What?" I ask, annoyed at being laughed at.

"It's a weird question."

"No it's not. It's a good one. Why are you so concerned with me and how I manage?"

"Because I'm a human being."

"I'm human and I don't care how you survive."

"Really? Is that why you ran out of your apartment after me this morning?"

He has me there. I don't feel like talking or thinking about that so I look away, scanning the crumbling buildings around us. There's no movement. No animals or otherwise. I remember enough about life before to know it should be weird but these days it's really not. There's not enough of us out here, dead or alive, to make a lot of noise.

"I just…" He hesitates, running his hand over his face once. "Don't get mad, but you're a girl. There aren't many women left around here and even fewer young, pretty ones. I worry what will happen if the wrong person sees you."

"I make it a point not to be seen."

"I see you."

I hold his eyes, seeing how golden they are in the

morning light. How warm.

"I made a mistake," I whisper.

"By helping me?" He doesn't sound hurt. Only curious.

I shake my head and shrug, looking away. I don't know. I don't regret helping him even with what it has cost me. I don't regret letting him into my home and letting him fill the empty space. I don't regret showing him the movie and the music. But most importantly I don't regret telling him to go.

"Promise not to get mad again?"

I laugh. "No."

"Okay. I'll say it anyway. Come with me."

I take a deep breath, knowing where this is going. It's going where it always goes when people find me, the lost little lamb out in the wild all alone. They want to save me. Years ago I would go with them. I would let them help me and I would watch them die and I would be alone all over again.

"I am coming with you. You're showing me your home," I say, dodging the request.

"You know what I mean. Come with me permanently. Stay with the gang. You'll be safer."

I snort a laugh. "Yeah right. You just said I'm at risk with all the men out here. Now you want me to move in with a mob of them. No thank you."

"I can keep you safe there."

"How? By claiming me? Making me yours and keeping me in your bed so I don't wind up pushed into someone else's? Or worse, passed around like a toy?"

He doesn't answer right away and I feel my blood boil.

"It wouldn't be like that. That's not what I'm suggesting," he finally says calmly. "I would never—

I'd never be a threat to you. I'd make sure no one else was either."

"No, thanks."

"I—" He takes a deep breath and lets it out harshly. "This all came out wrong."

"Hopefully, yeah. Look, I get it. You want to help me and I believe you. If you were willing to do something heinous you'd have done it last night. It would have been easy. But how is it a good idea to bring me somewhere that you have to protect me all the time? And what happens if you're gone? What if you die? Can I just walk out the door or do I belong to the gang then?"

He doesn't answer. That's it. I'm done because I'm right.

"I'm better off as I am."

"Yeah. Yeah, I guess you are," he says quietly. I can tell this really bothers him. He's sorry he can't help me and I hate that. I don't need help. I've got this. I've had it under control all on my own for years now and I don't need some knight in shining armor to come running up and save me.

As we walk in silence I see the park peek through between the buildings. The tall trees that have overrun the area waving in the light breeze. Crenshaw is in there. Crenshaw who has never offered me help beyond what I ask for. Who makes his trades with me, offers his advice when asked and then pisses off. Crenshaw who never calls me by my name.

"Thank you," I blurt out, surprising us both.

His brows pinch in confusion. "I thought you were mad at me. What are you thanking me for?"

"I am. I'm kinda mad at you. But you're being nice."

"You're mad at me for being nice?"

"No, I'm thanking you for being nice."

"I am so confused."

I grin at him. "Me too."

"Joss, I want you to understand that—"

"Shhhh! Shut up!" I whisper harshly, grabbing his arm and pulling him down into a crouch with me. "Look."

A deer. It's strolling slowly, almost casual, as though it doesn't have a care in the world. Not for zombies and certainly not for us.

"What do you want to do?" he whispers, leaning his head close. "Do you want to go for it?"

I nod excitedly. "I haven't had anything but rabbit in forever."

"Not stealthy enough to take down a deer?" he asks, smirking at me.

I glare at him. "Not alone, no, and neither are you. But if we work together…"

"I thought you don't play well with others."

I chuckle softly. "Ryan, for a chance at deer meat I can be very agreeable."

"I'll believe it when I see it. It's heading for the park. Let's cut over a block so we can run without spooking it."

We rise slowly out of our crouch, trying not to land in the deer's peripheral. Once we're clear of its sightline we take off at a sprint, running quietly down the street on the balls of our feet, landing on as little surface as possible to make the least amount of noise. We have to push through tall grass and dodge cars and rubble. Fallen street signs and sections of buildings. A refrigerator it looks like some idiots threw off a roof for fun. I wonder briefly, since we're in his neighborhood, if it was Ryan's band of idiots that did it.

When we reach the edge of the park we find that we beat the deer here. We quickly hide crouched down in a row of thick bushes just on the edge of the park where we can see the break in the trees where he's going to come in. I get impatient and stand up briefly, looking for him. He's walking so slowly I wonder if he's not sick. I don't want to eat rancid deer meat and get sick again. Food poisoning is deadly. I've only had to deal with it once. All I can say is thank goodness I had my toilet.

"Why is he moving so slowly?" I breathe as silently as I can.

"What should he be hurrying for? There's nothing chasing him."

"Not that he knows of."

"Maybe he's just a laid back guy."

"You two could hang out. Become bros."

He snorts quietly. "I need a good dinner more than a bro."

"Okay, he's in. I'll circle behind him on his right, you flank him on his left then we'll close in on him together. Good?"

"Good." Ryan stands up, his head and shoulders coming above the bushes. I stay crouched, ready to spring up like a sprinter out of the blocks. "Ready?"

"Ryan!" a voice bellows from behind us.

The deer jerks its head around, its ears twitching and its large black eyes scanning the area. Whether it spots us or the owner of the obnoxiously loud voice I don't know. It makes the smart choice and leaps into the thickness of the trees, disappearing into the shadows.

Ryan whirls around, looking for whoever is calling to him.

"Stay down," he mumbles.

"Duh," I reply, tucking myself farther into the bushes by his knees.

"Bray?" Ryan calls.

"Yeah, man, what are you doing?"

"Trying to catch some dinner. I was following a deer."

Bray laughs. "Come on. A deer? You're good but you're not that good."

"I'd be better if people didn't shout at the top of their lungs and scare it away."

"Sorry. I didn't know. I've been out looking for you all morning. We weren't sure we'd find you alive."

"You're not supposed to look for me."

"Yeah, I know. But with what happened with Kevin... Well, we made a decision to skip the rules a little and go looking for you at first light. We just lost him. No one was ready to lose you too."

A silence falls between them. I can see Ryan's hand clenching his knife tightly.

"But you gotta come in now," Bray tells him, breaking the silence. "Everyone needs to. Trent's in the crow's nest with the specs and he spotted bad news."

"What's up?"

"Risen. The dead, man, they're back in force."

"What? How?"

"Don't know, but we have theories. Trent has spotted at least fifty, probably more. And they're fresh."

Ryan curses under his breath. "Women and

70

children in the mix?"

"Yep. You get the idea of what's happened, right?"

A Colony has fallen.

"Colony," Ryan says darkly.

"That's what we think," Bray agrees. "It can't have been more than one and it can't have been one of the stadiums. The numbers would be higher. That means there's more of them out there than we know about."

"Unless the Risen are spread out. There might be more than Trent can see."

"We think there are. We're pretty sure it's just one section that's gone down though. A smaller one. We're hoping anyway. If all of the Colonies in the area get infected..."

"It'll be like the start of it all over again."

"Yeah. As it is it's dangerous to be out right now. We're going on lockdown until we get a better idea of how big this thing is going to get."

"Alright," Ryan says warily. "Let's get back."

Ryan flexes his hand and drops his knife into the soft grass beside me. I glance at it, then back up at him, wondering what the hell he's doing but he's already walking away. I watch and listen as their footsteps recede and he disappears from sight. I start counting, waiting it out, wondering how long I should give them to be out of sight entirely.

"What are you doing?!" I hear Bray call from far off.

"My knife!" Ryan calls back. He's close and getting closer. "I dropped it. Wait there, give me a minute!"

"Hurry up!"

Ryan runs back and drops down on his knees in front of me. His face is pinched in concern.

"You heard Bray?" he whispers.

I nod, my mouth pulled in a grim line.

"I should walk you back. It's not good to be out alone right now."

"You'll never shake this guy. Besides, I can make it. I've survived worse with less experience."

"I feel like a jerk just leaving you."

"You're not a jerk."

He grins. "That's the nicest thing you've ever said to me."

"Don't let it go to your head."

His face falls serious, his eyes searching mine.

"I'm gonna find you again," he says softly.

I smirk. "You can try."

I hope he understands. That he takes that statement for what it is. Permission, or at least as much as I can give. I want him to find me and, foolish as it may be, I know I'm going to make it easy.

"Ryan!" Bray shouts, sounding closer than before.

"Screw it," Ryan murmurs.

He crushes his lips to mine. A surprised whimper escapes the back of my throat, urging him on and suddenly his hands are on my face and in my hair. I grab his shoulders for support as he pulls me forward and off balance but then I'm pulling him to me. His chest presses against me as his lips soften and move slowly over mine. This is dangerous. His friend is close by, zombies are in high numbers again but I can't begin to care. It's my first kiss, quite possibly the only one I'll ever have so I let myself melt into him. I give up, I give in. I hold on and I enjoy the moment as the comet crash lands onto the earth and razes the entire world.

When he pulls away, his hands still in my hair and on my skin, his breathing is ragged. I, on the other hand, have stopped breathing entirely.

"Watch for me," he says roughly.

"What?"

He holds my face firmly in front of his, so close I can feel his breath on my skin. He locks eyes with me and repeats, "Watch for me. Keep your eyes open."

"I will," I whisper.

"Good." He lets go of my face and squeezes my hand briefly. "Be safe."

"You too."

He smiles at me one last time before he goes.

Then I'm alone again.

Chapter Seven

"Crenshaw!" I whisper loudly into the wilderness.

I'm standing in the thickest section of trees in the park turned forest, scanning the brush. I have to be careful because Crenshaw is a shifty old man who loves setting traps. Traps for food, traps for zombies, traps for people. I think the people traps are his favorite. Yep, there's a makeshift rope running up the inside of a tree. I'd bet my last sip of water that it's connected to a loop in the underbrush. I am not taking another step.

"Crenshaw!"

"I'm here," a disembodied voice calls from within the trees. He emerges from the shadows looking like Merlin if he'd fallen on hard times and got really into pot. He even has a staff for God's sake. "What do you need of me, Athena?"

Yeah, he calls me Athena, like the goddess of war. Years ago he said Joss was too mousey, that I was a survivor and deserved a survivor's name. He toyed with calling me Xena for a bit but I refused to respond to it. By the time we got to Athena, I just didn't care anymore.

"Nothing, I'm fine. I came to warn you that

there's been an outbreak in the Colonies. I've seen a lot more wraiths recently."

Wraiths, yes. That's what I said. I've entered into Mordor here.

"Ah, it was inevitable," he rasps. "The gates of Hell were bound to spring open again eventually. How many have escaped so far?"

"I'm not sure. I overhead some men talking and they've spotted at least fifty in the area. Probably more."

"You were in the company of men?"

"No, not really. I was in the park and I overheard them."

"And they didn't see you?" he asks skeptically. He's a crazy old bird but he's sharp. Irritatingly so.

"One of them might have known I was there," I admit grudgingly.

"Be careful."

"I'm always careful."

"Be doubly careful," he says, striking his staff on the ground twice for emphasis.

"Ok, yes. I'll be triple careful."

"You're sure you don't need anything of me? Tea? Food?" I shake my head, smiling at his generosity. "Water?"

Suddenly I'm reminded of Ryan's warning.

"Don't go to the watering holes," I blurt out.

He scowls at me, looking offended by the idea. "I never do. Why would I?"

"I don't know, but don't go there. The men also said that the holes are dangerous. That the Colonies are doing a lot of roundups there."

He watches me in silence for an uncomfortably long time, his face entirely devoid of emotion.

"These men," he finally says slowly, "they said an awful lot, didn't they?"

I shrug, trying to look unconcerned. "They were chatty."

"All of this while you were in earshot."

"Chatty and stupid."

"No one alive today is stupid, Athena."

I roll my eyes, getting tired of the interrogation or accusation. Whatever this is it's wearing on me. People in general are wearing on me and I think I've had *way* too much interaction recently. I need to detox.

"What do you want me to say? What do you want from me?" I ask, letting my frustration show.

"I want you to be careful."

"And I said I would. I will be. I always am."

"What is more dangerous than the wraiths?" He asks it like a condescending school teacher and I have to suppress a groan. I've heard this lecture a million times.

"Snakes?"

"Athena."

"People. Living, breathing, thieving people."

"Remember it well," he warns. Then he steps back, blending into the shadows. It's very theatrical and I wonder if he practices when I'm not around.

"You try and watch out for people," I grumble, heading for the exit. I'm wondering how giving him a heads up ended with me being scolded. I want out of the woods, out of the park, out of the whole city. Out of this mess entirely.

I'm debating what to do about dinner tonight and which water supply to tap when it happens. An early warning system goes off. From a tree about a block and a half down a massive flock of birds takes to the sky. Aside from the beating of their wings they don't make a sound. No cawing. No screeching. They're not freaking out over the dead so what are they running from? It's something human or another animal. If it's an animal it's big. Threatening. If it's human they're not used to treading softly and only one type of person nowadays hasn't finely honed their creeping skills. They don't have to. They live behind fences and walls and sleep on mattresses and sheets and wash their hair with real soap, not with some beige bar made in Merlin's Magical Shop of Wonders in the woods.

Colonists.

I hide myself deep in the bushes, close to where I was hiding with Ryan. As my breathes come in short and painful I feel so far removed from Crenshaw's Athena or Ryan's jerk Joss. Now I'm Jocelyn, eight years old and terrified, hiding behind a tree while evil closes in on me. I can pretend to be as tough as I want but the person who knows the truth is the only one who matters; me. I know every single day how scared I really am. How tired, how angry, how lonely. It doesn't matter what anyone else thinks or if I work my butt off to make sure there is no 'anyone else' around to see it. It's still true. I'm still scared.

I don't have to wait long for the silent, silver electric car to come rolling by at a ridiculously slow speed. Most roads are cracked, sprouting weeds and grass or filled with stripped out cars and debris but there's a trail cleared that winds through the area. It's something some of the gangs have done or maybe the Colonists did it? I'm not sure. Either way, areas on this trail are the marketplace for the crews who are willing to barter with one another. The morning after a new moon you can find them gathering at random locations along this road to trade goods and act like morons together. I've obviously never attended but I've watched from the roof before and, if I'm being honest, I've watched with a little envy. Most of the Lost Boys get along, laughing and shouting together. Like friends.

But now the roads are empty and silent, barely a sound coming from the ridiculously small, shiny car gliding through this derelict world. It doesn't belong here. *They* don't belong here. The sight of a car, something that was once so common place and now so nauseatingly strange, sends chills down my spine. I feel cold sweat break out over my clammy skin and I remind myself to breath evenly.

They can't hear me. They can't see me. They don't know I'm here. They will not take me.

I try to tell myself to calm down. I doubt they're doing a roundup right now, not without their vans with the doors that lock from the outside. It's not really a good time anyway, not for anybody. All of us in the wild, those with any sense at least, are holed up in our homes waiting to see just how bad this latest outbreak is going to get. If any sense of responsibility still existed in the world the Colonists would be out here to kill these things off once and for all. Clean up their mess. But there isn't and that's not why they're here. They're here to make a point. To let us know that not all of them have fallen, not everyone in their golden city is infected. To warn us not to come looting.

You better believe that if they ever did fail entirely those of us in the wild would descend upon their stocks like vultures. I dream about it at night when I'm not having nightmares about crawlers eating my legs. I don't wish them ill, I'm not hoping they all die, I just want to take their stuff. Is that bad? I don't even know anymore. This type of moral questioning wasn't covered in *The Breakfast Club*. I fear the structure of my upbringing is noticeably lacking.

***

The next week is a bear. My life, already more than a little stressful, gets way worse. The biggest, most notable source of my anxiety is the fact that I haven't moved. I can't. The zombie threat is back and bigger than it has been in years leaving me thinking that the numbers Ryan's friend quoted were conservative. There are definitely more than fifty dead bloating the ranks out there. In the middle of the night I can hear the groaning outside breaking the silence I hadn't realized I'd grown accustomed to. This is the old days, the early days. The bad days.

My other problem is the Colonists. They're everywhere. The trucks and vans are out patrolling the streets and blaring over the loudspeakers again, something they haven't done in long time. They play up the threat of the dead, telling us the only place to be safe from this latest outbreak is in their compounds. Are we idiots out here? They must think so because we all know where the fresh dead came from and the idea that we'd be safer where the infection found footing again is laughable. It's also infuriating.

"Go to Hell!"

I freeze, shocked by the unfamiliar sound of human life outside my windows. I can feel pins and needles prickling under my skin as I run to the window, sticking to the shadows cast by the late afternoon sun. From this height I can see the street a block over, looking down over the lower buildings to the east. The Colonist trucks are there. Three of them.

I watch as Lost Boys run at the vehicles, weapons raised. There are at least ten of them, a decent gathering, but I worry. Word is, if Crenshaw's sources are good, that the Colonists still have guns, though I've never seen or heard them used. The Lost Boys attack, swinging weapons that look long, dark and deadly. I hear indiscernible shouts, words lost in the wind or the distance. Or in rage. Maybe they never meant anything other than anger.

The Colonists are spilling out of the vehicles to defend themselves and I wonder if they have anyone locked inside. They collide with the gang and the shouts intensify. The clang of metal against metal, screams of pain and more curses carry over otherwise silent streets and up to my fractured window. I watch carefully, trying to make out the shape of the men. The color of their hair. I'm holding the softened, rotted wood of the window frame with white knuckles and I'm wondering, worrying, if Ryan is with them.

There's a flash of orange light. Fire. The Lost Boys have lit a torch. Or I think it's a torch until it flies through the air and lands at the rear tire of the trail vehicle. It explodes into an inferno, crawling up the side of the van like a spider, spinning a web of heat and smoke behind it. More cries ring out from both sides and the men disentangle themselves from each other as the fire becomes the true threat to everyone. The gang retreats, quickly gathering a fallen member from the ground and dragging him away. A trail of red mars the ground behind him, appearing especially bright and red over a patch of yellow, dry grass.

The fire is coming for it. It consumes everything,

devouring the van and burning brightly over nearly the entire surface. The Colonists pile into their remaining two vehicles and quickly pull away, leaving the fallen van to burn itself out. Within the space of three minutes the confrontation is over. The only signs it ever took place are fire and red grass, both of which are burning away, flaming out. They leave behind only a pillar of dark smoke in the sky and a black stain on the ground. And I wonder again, as I watch it all burn, if they had anyone locked inside.

Chapter Eight

The fight has me freaked. I wait it out another two days after that but eventually I absolutely have to leave the building for more food and water. It hasn't rained in days meaning my emergency bucket is dry. I'm also a little worried about Crenshaw being down at ground level with all of this going on. He's much more at risk than I am and I know I need to make a kill or go fishing in the bay. I have to bring him some meat soon because he won't do it himself.

Gathering an empty jug for water, my knife and ASP, I curse myself for never learning to use a bow and arrow. It'd be nice to shoot a meal instead of chasing it down, tackling it and slitting its throat. Have you ever chased a wild rabbit? How 'bout a squirrel? No, you haven't because it's exhausting and nearly futile. But it's also necessary. I've been trapped in this apartment with nothing but carrots, potatoes and tomatoes for over a week and I'm not a vegetarian. Not at heart.

When I step outside into the unseasonably warm winter sun my hands are slick with sweat. I'm nervous. This is dangerous, more so than it has been for years. I wonder if I've still got the skills to survive this world.

What if I've gone soft? What if I can't handle as many dead as I used to? How fast can I run these days?

My thoughts and doubts are stopped in their tracks along with my feet when I round the corner. I'm shocked. Stunned. Afraid. Excited.

There across the street on the side of a building just a block and a half from my home is writing on a wall.

Welcome to the apocalypse.

My shoulders fall, relief coursing through me. Surprising me. It's Ryan, it has to be. I wonder if he knows I didn't move or if it was wishful thinking. A shot in the dark to see if he gets a reaction. To see if I forgive him and trust him enough to stay. I didn't think I knew the answer to either of those questions but the fact that I'm still here is answer enough. It'd be dangerous for me to move right now with the rise in the number of dead. With the Colonists out going door to door like they're selling religion. It'd suck but if I really felt threatened I'd have done it. Yet I haven't.

What's really important here, what makes me heave a shaky sigh of relief, is that he's alive. He's unhurt.

Or is he?

I've been in my home for over a week. I have no way of knowing when this message was written. Was it before or after the confrontation I saw two days ago? I can't know, not with certainty. So it means nothing. And it shouldn't. It shouldn't mean anything anyway. He's not my concern. What I need to worry about right now is not some vague message scrawled out in brick dust, something that will wash away with the first heavy rain. My worries are more substantial and far more urgent.

I put the message out of my mind, get my head in the game and move on.

Three hours later Crenshaw and I have lunch. It's a mangy little rabbit that ran me all over hell and back but I got him in the end. Crenshaw, in a very rare show of friendship, asks me to stay and eat with him. He has a system for smoking the meat, making it not only delicious but also keeping a low profile while cooking. Even though I'm worried he'll get a visit from one of the Lost Boys while I'm here I take the chance for a shot at a good, hot meal. Also, and I keep this to myself, I don't mind the idea of the company so much either.

"You look as a true warrior, Athena," he says, pulling his robe more tightly around himself as he leans down to stoke the fire. It's a real robe, like a bathrobe. There are sailboats on it. Blue ones.

My hands and clothes are soaked in blood from killing and skinning the rabbit. I'm tired, scratched up from branches, bushes and bunny claws and I'm sure I look more nuts than anything else. Does that make me a warrior? I doubt it. I think I'd have to be afraid of a lot less to be classified as one.

"Really? I was thinking I needed a bath."

He snorts at me. "Your generation is obsessed with cleanliness. Do you think even the Kings and Queens in medieval court were so thoroughly bathed? I assure you they were not."

"I don't know, Cren," I say doubtfully, looking down at myself. "I think I've gone beyond royalty filth and moved into cavewoman status."

"It's good for you."

I smile as I take a seat at his table. "You're the doctor."

He ignores me as he cooks. I enjoy the feeling of not being alone but being left alone. It's a strangely wonderful sensation. It's cozy here in this earth and mud hut that's he built. It's small, my leg is pressing against his cot tucked in the far corner, and it's incredibly dark inside but it fits him. Outside this sparse living quarter is his real home; his garden. It's all hidden deep in the brush and trees of the park but it's expansive as well. If he asked me to go out and get him something from it I wouldn't know where to begin. It all looks like a jungle to me but to him it's perfectly clear.

He brings me a plate with my smoked rabbit on it and sits across from me.

"Have you seen your friend lately?" he asks casually.

I stiffen. "I don't have friends, remember?"

"Athena."

I groan. "Don't do that. Don't scold me. I talked to him once. It's no big deal and it's not a friendship."

He chews thoughtfully. "If you speak to him again—"

"I'm never going to see him again," I interrupt. I immediately wish I hadn't. Crenshaw stares down his nose at me. I cave. "I'm sorry, please continue."

He clears his throat. "If you speak to him again, be wary but cordial."

My rabbit slips through my fingers and plops on my plate. "Cordial? You want me to be nice to him? Since when?"

"Since the wraiths outnumber us again."

"I don't know that they outnumber us," I say

doubtfully.

"Since the Colonists walk these woods."

I drop my meat again, this time intentionally. "They've been here? Near you?"

He watches me calmly. "Not near enough to see but near enough for me to hear. Do not worry for me."

"Crenshaw—"

"I said do no worry, Athena. I have shrouded my home. I will remain unseen."

"Shrouded it with what? A spell?"

He frowns at me, looking at me like I've gone mad. "With camouflage."

"Right, sorry."

Sometimes I forget that Crenshaw's crazy is selective. He'll be telling me one minute to burn sage to ward off evil spirits and the next he'll be asking if I remember the football Thanksgiving episode of Friends. It's hit or miss. More often miss.

Eventually I say goodbye to Master Gandalf and carefully pick my way out of his neck of the woods. I'm full of good food, sedated by whatever incense he was burning in that hut but my day is only half done. Now the hard part. I have to climb to the top of one of my buildings to get fresh water.

This is dangerous for two—wait, no three… I guess actually four—it's dangerous for a whole lot of reasons, let's just go with that. Colonists, zombies, Lost Boys, bears. Yes! I have seen a bear before. I cannot tell you how scary that was. He was huge and hungry and fast. I only got away because I climb way better than he could. I ended up sleeping in an unfamiliar building out on the fire escape until he got bored or hungry and finally left.

I decide to minimize my danger factor since I'm

already tired from Elmer Fuddin' it after that rabbit. I go to my closest water source. It's five blocks away and to the south, the opposite direction of Ryan's home. At least I know I'm walking away from one threat I'd like to hide from. The walk there shows me how flooded the world really is. It's one thing to see it from up high and it's another entirely to get down in it. Every corner I round seems to bring me nearly face to face with a Risen. I'm able to carefully avoid them, eventually going to the rooftops to do so, but that's dangerous and kind of lazy on my part. I just want to get my water and go home when what I should be doing is putting them down and eliminating the problem for Future Joss. Making Future Joss's life easier with less zombies to face on a daily basis. But that's Future Joss's issue and right now Present Joss isn't feeling it.

Selfishness, especially my own, is what makes this place so hard to survive.

When I get to the building I have a choice to make. Go inside and take the stairs or climb the fire escape. The fire escape of course sounds like the better option because I won't have to be inside a building that for all I know could be crawling with Risen. It's the smart choice on paper. But when you look at the situation more closely, mainly at the bolts securing the fire escape to the building, you see the flaws in the plan. It's been many moons, many winters, many rain storms since this thing was deemed safe by the local fire inspector and I know for a fact that it's hanging on by a thread. As I stand here on the sidewalk examining it, feeling more exposed by the second, I see the structure shift in the wind. I'm not setting foot on that.

Inside it is.

My skin crawls at the thought. I have to take several deep breaths to psyche myself up for this. Once I'm inside, I'm all stealth and speed. I don't need to be a hero here. I'm not looking to hunt zombies tonight and help decrease the surplus population, no matter how much Future Joss will be annoyed by it. What I need to do is get in and get out without contact – living or otherwise.

But what I need, what I want and what I get have rarely lined up.

That Cabbage Patch Doll with the blood in her blond hair? I wanted a brunette.

I also wanted my parents to live past New Years.

Do you see the pattern here?

What I see is a Risen at the end of the hall by the door to the stairs. The *only* door to the stairs.

"Great," I mutter, pulling out the ASP with my left hand and unsheathing my knife with my right.

I'm right handed and my preferred weapon here is the ASP. So why am I holding it in my weak hand? Because it doesn't need me to be strong. Not really. It doesn't need me to be accurate either. All it needs is a target and a little momentum and that thing will crush bone under its steel tip like it's nothin'. Like cracking a walnut. Ryan was right to be jealous. This thing is amazing. I sleep with it like a toddler with a teddy bear.

A brisk breeze flutters through the smashed door behind me and carries down the hall. Almost instantly the hunchback female with a serious skin condition is aware of me. She begins the slow shamble down the long hall toward me and I think about waiting for her, making her come to me and maybe even drawing her out into the street before engaging her. But the day is waning, light will be scarce soon and I'm not about to be caught out in the wild after hours.

I move down the hall slowly, checking doors as I go and keeping my eyes on her progress. When my beauty queen with the gray skin sloughing off her bones moans into range I kneel down and swing out, aiming for her shin. It cracks, breaking the bone and dropping her to the ground. Once she's down I quickly kick her over on her side, making her temple more accessible. I could have hit her in the head when she was up but it wouldn't have ended her. It would only have either made a mess of her face or been a waste of energy. The top of the human skull, the only section I have clean access to in this tight hallway, is incredibly strong. The temple and the face - not so much.

She grabs at my leg, clawing at the denim and moaning. Her big dead eyes are looking right at me and it's that more than anything else that gives me chills. How is she looking at me with those things? What does she even see?

"Nothing," I growl, growing angry at her constant moaning. At her greedy hands. "You don't see anything."

I swing the ASP down hard, making contact with her cheek bone. It explodes in a rush of black and gray. A tooth pops out of her mouth and skitters across the floor behind me. I bring the baton down again, this time closer to her ear. I must catch the temple a little because she stops moving. I don't. I keep swinging the baton because I can. Because I want her gone. I want all semblance of a human face to be beaten into the floor and stripped from this body because it's not real anymore. It's not human and it shouldn't look like one. No one should come through here to find her finally, perfectly, wholly dead and think how sad it is.

When my arm grows tired and I'm sufficiently grossed out by the softness of what I'm now beating, I stop. I'm breathing heavy. I'm tired. I'm tired of a lot of things. I need to get upstairs, get my water and get home. I'll clean myself up and watch a movie, something I haven't done in a week. Not since Ryan rode the bike. I don't know why I haven't but tonight for some reason I really desperately want to.

I take off at a sprint, ignoring the rest of the doors in the hallway. I don't have enough time, patience or daylight to mind them all. It's risky but not as risky as being out at night. This building is only six stories. I'm rounding the corner on the stairs heading up to the fifth floor, breathing deep and even, searching for my calm again, when I trip. I fly forward, my momentum thrusting me up the stairs and onto the fifth floor landing. I watch with horrified interest as my ASP, my greatest, most loyal friend, flies down the hall without me.

"Ah, hell," I groan.

There's another groan behind me. I scurry quickly up the last two stairs. When I spin around to look behind me I want to scream. It's a crawler. A no leg having, teeth at your toes, scare the bejeezus out of me crawler. I hate these things. I hate them for the very situation that I'm in right now – they come out of nowhere. Taking a zombie down on purpose in order to end them the way I just did, that's one thing. But Risen like this guy who slither across the earth at your feet like a snake, that's messed up.

He's coming for me now, reaching up and pulling himself with that incredible, undeterred by pain zombie strength that he has. He's on the landing with me before I can think to move. Then his hand is on my ankle. I kick at his face with my free foot, making contact with his nose and breaking it violently. It makes a sick, satisfying *crunch* sound but it doesn't stop him. I pull myself backwards, reaching for the ASP with desperate fingers. He's climbing my leg. His hand is on my knee, bringing his face level with my foot. I have the terrifying thought that he'll bite it through the worn material of my tennis shoe.

I finally grip the base of the baton and bring it around, crashing it into his forearm. I repeat the process until he finally lets me go because he has to. The bone is broken. I crabwalk away from him without thinking and I end up in a room. It looks like it used to be an office of some kind. I back into a heavy metal desk that refuses to move, to give me room to escape. I'm trapped. And he's coming, pulling himself into the room after me using his one functioning arm and groaning incessantly.

I quickly lash out with my foot, swinging the heavy wood door closed on his face. He's too far into the room, though. I only succeed in slamming it against his skull. It bounces back at me as he continues to groan. Feeling frustrated, angry and scared I kick again. The door smacks him in the skull, pinning his head between it and the frame. I kick again and again and again, beating his head between the two sections of wood. I'm kicking over and over, hoping it's enough. That eventually I'll hit that sweet spot on his temple just wrong, just hard enough to kill and he'll go down for good.

Kick, crunch! Kick, crunch! Kick, crunch!

There's a heavy, blessed crack. I know I've gotten my wish. I kick one last time and let the door swing back at me after it makes mushy contact with what's left of his head. I don't look at the mess I've made. It's nothing I haven't seen before but I do want to be able to eat later and actually enjoy it so I stand up slowly on shaking legs and step quickly over what's left of the guy.

Today, I have emphatically decided, is for suck.

And it's not over. This day is never ending. I still haven't scored my water and I just worked up quite a thirst with my leg workout back there. I take a moment to calm down, to breathe easy and remind myself to be careful when what I really want to do is run through this building as fast as I can, get my water from the roof and run back out again. Time efficient, but deadly. So I don't do it.

Turns out I needn't have worried. I make it to the roof without further incident but when I arrive my heart sinks. The door, which I normally keep latched firmly, is thrown wide open. Someone has been here. I pass through the opening slowly, scanning the open space and hoping against hope that I don't run into the living.

I luck out. There's only a Risen. She's wandering around aimlessly on the far side of the roof opposite my rain system. I'm tired and grumpy so I ignore her and her pencil skirt office attire for now. Maybe I won't have to engage her at all.

I move quickly to my rain barrels which are actually Rubbermaid rectangular storage containers, the kind people used to put holiday decorations in and shove in a dark corner of their garage 90% of the year. Now they sit attached to a series gutters I ripped off the sides of buildings and secured to each other so they run side by side, creating several long lines of water collection that feed down into a pasta strainers I fit in the lid of each tub. They keep leaves and other debris out, including frogs, but I'll still have to boil it when I get home just to be sure there's no bacteria. Or I would have to do that if there were any water in the tubs.

They've cleaned me out. Whoever they were they took my entire water supply from this roof. I throw the lid off each tub even though I can tell from just nudging them with my foot that they're empty. Every last one of them.

"Dammit!"

All of that for nothing. The zombie in the hall, the crawler in the door, this one coming at me now here on the roof. All of it. All for nothing. I risked everything and now I'm going home empty handed.

I kick each tub across the roof and watch as one trips and tumbles over the edge. It stuns me for half a second, just long enough to think it's a bad thing. Then I flip a switch and think it's the best thing ever. I grab the gutter work and launch it over the edge as well, chuckling when I hear it clatter loudly to the ground. I'm breathing quickly and feeling crazy. I'm so angry, something I haven't felt in forever. I got a taste of it when Ryan dropped into my world and blew it up but this is different. This is frustration and rage. It's pent up for miles and I don't know what to do with it. What I should do, healthy or not, is stow it. Now is not the time for this.

I drop the other gutter fixture I was holding in my hand and let it fall carelessly to the rough rooftop. Watching the Risen girl come at me I can't bring the numb. I can't find the calm that I strove for on the way up here and barely managed. I need it to do this right, to make sure I survive and keep my head on straight, but it just won't come. I back up as she stalks me slowly and clumsily. I let her walk me to the brink. The backs of my legs hit the lip that rises above the edge by just a few feet, just enough to trip a person and send them tumbling down to their death. It's a dangerous feature. I wonder how that ever made it in the pearly white, disinfected, overly sanitized safety net world that existed ten years ago.

Look out! Coffee is hot!
Knives are sharp!
This End Up, numbnuts!

This woman is older than me by at least twenty years and deader by about four. She didn't make it. All of her warning labels were gone and the world was too much for her to figure out on her own.

Beware: Zombies bite!

I'm not ashamed to say I feel superior to this chick. She has years of experience on me but I survived and she didn't. She may have had a 401K, a husband and an Audi, but at least I still have a heartbeat. One that's thrumming wildly in my chest as my breath comes hot, hard and fast into my lungs.

It's all of these emotions, all these things I've forgotten and gotten on without that are now literally bursting through me, seeping from my pores and smothering me from the inside out. There's so much, too much.

And it's gotta go somewhere.

When Corporate Kelly makes her big move and lunges for me I drop down to the ground on my knees and spring forward. I tackled her at the thighs, standing up when I make contact and lifting her bony body onto my shoulder. Then I push on her knees and flip her forward, over my back and over the edge. I send her off the roof face first to kiss the pavement below. And I turn to watch it happen. I wait for the impact and when the *smack!* echoes back up to me, I throw my arms in the air to signal a touchdown.

If that move doesn't get me the Heisman then justice is dead.

I'm still pissed about my water, or lack of, when I get back to my neighborhood. I've still got some rabbit, though, and some veggies that I can eat raw instead of boiling. And I still have a home to go back to, so that's a plus. I haven't been ratted out yet just as I dared to instill a little faith in humanity again. Of course that's over now that humanity stole my stuff, mainly my life sustaining resource. But that's okay because Ryan's different and I actually choose to believe that.

It's then that I decide I need to know if he's alive.

I make a detour home that takes me longer but it also takes me by the wall. I look at his message for a moment, wondering what to say back. I think of a hundred things that I immediately cast off as stupid, lame, boring, too obscure or too suggestive.

And then it starts to rain. There's no prelude to it, no soft pitter patter of tiny first drops leading the way. No, it downpours from moment one, soaking me to the bone in a matter of seconds. On the bright side my rain bucket upstairs will be full in no time and I will have fresh water. On the dark side, the one that seethes inside my soul and throws zombies off rooftops as part of a stress management system, I'm reminded yet again that my adventure was all for nothing. I nearly died multiple times and all for not. It's not a new thing in my life, I'm just painfully aware of it right now. As I am painfully aware of a lot of things lately.

Finally inspired, I pick up the brick on the ground, cross out a part of his message and write one word of my own. It's not pretty and it's not poetic, but it is honest.

~~Welcome to~~ *the apocalypse* **blows.**

When I wake up in the morning I still can't find the calm. The numb. The tap out I need in order to be the me that survives. It's troubling and I blame Ryan. One more thing on the poor guy's shoulders, I know, but credit where credit is due. This is his fault. I thought about telling him as much last night on the wall.

You gave me the sickness.

I don't know a lot but I know enough to know that sounds dirty. I don't know how he'd take it, I'm not sure what types of books he's been reading, but I doubt it would have been interpreted as I meant it.

I give it another day before I decide I feel enough like myself to be trusted in the outside world. I spend my time indoors watching *The Breakfast Club* and letting myself laugh audibly. It feels weird but I like it. And when the credits roll I'm still smiling because I noticed something about this movie that I've never noticed before, even after countless watchings: I can relate.

I am a brain.

An athlete.

A basket case.

A princess.

A criminal.

And when I step outside and cruise past the wall, expecting to find it washed clean of our small

scribblings, I notice something else.
    I'm no longer alone.

Put down a Z in your name today.
Bringing you a better world, one kill at a time.

Chapter Nine

I'm scared of spiders. I scream like a girl.

I'm scared of clowns. I'm glad they're all dead.

What about a crawler clown?

You're the devil. I'll have nightmares for months.

I could come stay with you. Keep the clowns away…

Stay away from me, dipshit. I have spiders and I know how to use them.

I'm the King of the Dipshits!

We're writing almost every day now. I feel like

it's getting dangerous. It's dangerous for us to develop a routine that the Colonists can track. It's dangerous to leave these messages in my neighborhood that anyone can see. It's dangerous to have him sneaking here to write them because eventually someone will see him do it. It's dangerous to have my back turned, unguarded, as I write stupid things to a guy I've only met once and should have walked away from at the start.

But I didn't and everything has changed because of it.

I'm crouched down under a tree, waiting like a snake in the grass for a bird to leave her nest so I can steal her eggs, when I hear him. His voice rings out, echoing through the park and resonating in my ears. It startles both me and the bird, alerting it to threats in the area and I lose all hope of scoring those eggs today. That boy cannot help but mess up my world.

It's been a month since the night I met Ryan and I'm surprised that I recognize his voice immediately. He's in the far side of the park near where we ran into his friend Bray. I crane my neck to look for him. What I see first is a tall, thin blond guy a few years older than I am. He's somewhere in his twenties with a weathered face and sharp eyes. I sink back down low, scurrying silently into a patch of tall grass and ferns. I'm hiding from him. I don't realize it until I've already done it but I'm glad. His eyes make me nervous. I watch through the patchy green blur of leaves and blades as he moves languidly through the brush, barely rustling it as he walks. Beside him is another unfamiliar face, an older man with dark hair, probably somewhere in his forties. He's moving with far less care, almost crashing through the grass and chuckling with his head bent down. He's laughing with Ryan.

I can see him now. He's slightly behind the other two, walking farthest from me near a bank of trees. He passes in and out of shadows under the canopy of the foliage, the sunlight shining on his dark hair, brightening it then losing it to blackness. When he glances my way, looking at the older man beside him, he's smiling broadly.

I feel a small pang. An itch in my chest that I can't understand and I can't scratch.

They keep thundering through the forest; Ryan, the older man and the lithe footed guy with the freaky eyes. I follow them. This, I acknowledge, is stupid. But I'm seventeen and I've never done a stupid thing in my adult life. I figure I'm long past due. Besides, that pang in my chest will not be denied.

Eventually the tall blond holds up his hand, says something inaudible to the other two. They quickly scatter. They fan out to create a triangle around a small area of low lying grass just at the edge of the trees. In under a minute I can't see or hear any of them. It makes me sick to my stomach to see it because I realize I could come walking through this area and cruise right past all of them, never knowing they were there. Not until it's too late. Suddenly I wonder if I haven't done that already. Do they already know about me? Have I been spotted before?

My hands are clammy and my heart begins skipping painfully in my chest.

Odds are I have been. I'm stealthy, clever and quick, but there are a lot of eyes in this area. It's unrealistic to believe I've gone unnoticed by all of them. I sit and fret about this until my legs go numb but I don't move. I can't move, not until they're gone. I've gotten myself into this situation and now I have to wait it out. They're obviously hunting and their patience is impressive. And annoying. I wish they'd get bored and move on already.

Then I see what they're waiting for. Moving into the clearing with great caution is a buck. He's tall and broad. A big, hulking, powerful package of meat and deliciousness that has my mouth watering just looking at him. I've seen old advertisements in decrepit, broke down fast food joints. I know what used to make people drool. It was the end product. The final presentation of a piece of meat after countless ugly, messy and thoroughly disturbing things happened to it all at the hands of someone or something else. Tell me the phrase 'mechanically separated chicken' doesn't send a chill down your spine. I read it on a bag of dry dog food once (yes, I ate the dog food) and I almost gagged at the thought. Not on the dog food, though. That was tasty.

What I'm saying is that my idea of delicious is so much broader than it used to be. It's more big picture and the big picture right now is an 8 point buck with a body full of finger lickin' good.

I wait anxiously as the buck saunters into the clearing, munching on grass and occasionally surveying his surroundings. I'm surprised he doesn't smell the Lost Boys sitting so close by or hear one breathing. The fact that none of them have coughed, yawned or even swallowed too loudly is amazing to me. I guess because I don't see them hiding from others the way I have to. All I see them do is walk through the world like they own the place and I assume they aren't any good at sneaking. But today I stand, or sit with dead legs, corrected.

Suddenly the blond guy is on top of the buck. It happens so fast and is so unexpected I actually gasp. The buck is just as startled as I am. Probably more so. He goes to run but the guy has a hold on him and they both stumble slightly. Ryan and the older guy grab onto the buck as well. The thing puts up a hell of a fight, ducking his head down and using his sharp horns to keep the men at bay. Ryan takes a point to the arm and I watch as red blood blossoms on his shirt. He doesn't slow down though and I'm not even sure he can feel it through the adrenaline. They struggle with the buck, almost losing it at one point before the older guy grabs onto the thing's hind legs above the knee. He's taking hooved feet to the shins which I know will bruise for days but he holds on. There are shouts and cries, grunts and panic, but then it all goes silent. The buck collapses to the ground. I look around in surprise, wondering what did it.

Until I see the blood. It's fanning out over the green grass making it look shiny and wet like it just rained. Only it's red. Vibrant and angry red. And there's the sharp eyed guy standing in front of it, dripping red knife in hand, blood splatter across his shirt, neck and face, and he's grinning. He's grinning down at the expired animal at his feet and the light in his eyes and the knife in his hand make my blood run cold.

***

I don't tell Ryan that I saw him. I don't tell Crenshaw either. Ryan would be excited, Crenshaw would be mad and at this point I don't even know how

I feel about it so I keep it to myself. I'm good at that.

What I do tell both of them is that I've seen a lot of Colonists lately. The zombies are still in full force but I'm getting used to that again. It seems like they've always been there. An omnipresent threat that I can put in the back of my mind and deal with on auto pilot. They're dumb and predictable and I don't even have to kill them if they see me. If I'm tired or loaded down with supplies, I have no problem evading a Risen and letting them keep on shuffling. All it takes most of the time is crossing the street. Crisis averted. Zombies were a big problem in the beginning when everyone and their mother was becoming one but now with the humanity herd thinned down to those of us who can survive it and the number of people in the area outnumbering the zombies, I don't worry about it nearly as much. Probably not as much as I should.

But right now my biggest worry is the Colonists and their recruitment tactics. It's been a month since the rise in the zombie population thanks to the loss of one of their Colonies. After the fight and fire I saw in the street they stopped with the helping hand routine and went back to rounding people up like strays. I've warned Crenshaw, though he met the news with his usual disinterest and sage, wizardly advice:

"Luck favors the prepared," he intoned, swaying his staff back and forth like the swinging pendulum of a clock. I'm pretty sure he meant to hypnotize me. "Keep thy blade and wits sharp."

Spoken like a fortune cookie from Frodo's kitchen.

I left a message for Ryan the other day warning him as well.

Colonists are the new plague.

Watch your back.

Don't I know it.
Do you nee

His message is cut off. My heart slams to a halt. That's all he wrote. He must have been interrupted but by what? A Risen? A Colonist? Another Lost Boy? There are so many possibilities of what could have gone wrong that I feel helpless trying to figure out what happened to him. And I am not the helpless type. It actually occurs to me to go to his gang. It's ridiculous and so stupid but I seriously consider it. I can watch from afar for a little while, see if I can see him coming and going. And if I can't? I don't know. I don't know what I'll do then. This is the second time I've been worried for his life in a very short amount of time and I wonder what exactly it is I'm doing here. And for what? A little conversation on a wall and the memory of broad shoulders and brown eyes? Yeah, I feel less lonely and I feel a lot more of a lot of other things I'd forgotten existed, but to what end? How many of my old rules am I gonna break over this? And where does it stop? When I'm dead? It makes me sick just thinking about it but I can't let this go. I can't let him go.

I'm hurrying past the wall, heading toward his part of town, when warm hands reach out from the shadows of a darkened doorway and yank me back. I don't scream. I don't panic. I'm conditioned well beyond all of that. As I'm falling backward, my back slamming into someone else's front, I reach for my knife. I'm spinning it deftly in my hand just as an arm encircles my waist and a hand covers my mouth. That's fine. That's good, waste that constraint to smother a cry for help I never intended to loose. All the more room for me to swing out my arm, bring it back hard and drive my blade deep inside my captors gut. He'll bleed out for hours from a wound like that. That is if the zombies don't scent him first.

"Joss," he breathes in my ear.

I halt my arm just in time, just as the tip of my knife is pressing into his flesh.

"Whoa, whoa, whoa," Ryan says quickly, feeling the prick of my knife. "Jesus, Joss, don't stab me."

"Dunf creen ab vee," I growl against his hand. I'm breathing hard through my nose, my adrenaline spiked and coursing like lightning through my veins. I can feel his chest rising and falling against my back. It's slow and even.

"I know, I'm sorry I grabbed you," he apologizes in a whisper, somehow understanding my angry muffle speak. "If I let you go, will you scream?"

"I erfer seen."

"No," he chuckles softly. "I guess you wouldn't. I'm letting go. Please don't stab me."

He releases me in one quick motion like he's releasing a wild animal. His hands go up in defense and he takes a step back when I round on him, knife still ready in my hand.

"If I was going to stab you, you'd already be dead. Or dying," I say, my voice tense but quiet.

He smiles. "I believe it."

"What are you doing here? Why did you grab me?"

"I heard a Colonist truck coming by a little while ago."

My eyes shoot to the street, scanning what I can see of it. As far as I can tell it's clear.

"It's gone," Ryan assures me. "I was writing you a message when I heard it so I hid in here. Even after it left, though, I was worried it could come back. I was worried you'd be writing back to me when it did."

"So you waited for me?"

"Yeah."

"That was stupid."

He snorts, shaking his head. "You're welcome."

"You're staying out in the open for too long. What if a Risen wandered by? You have that cut on your arm and—"

"How do you know about that?"

I stop and berate myself for being the stupid one.

"I was there. In the woods. I saw you guys take the buck down."

He grins at me looking proud. "You saw that? Pretty good, right?"

I shrug, looking away. "You got hurt doing it, so it wasn't that impressive."

"You're cold. And jealous. Trent's an amazing hunter. You should dream of having half his skills."

"Which one was Trent? The tall guy?"

"Yeah. He's our main lookout. He's usually parked in the crow's nest but we pull him out for hunting now and then because he's just so freakishly good at it. He hears and sees everything."

"Yeah, I believe it," I mutter, remembering his eyes. I feel uncomfortable all of the sudden. I feel watched.

"So, hey, my message wasn't finished. I was

going to ask if you need anything. Are you doing okay?"

I frown at him. "I'm fine. I can take care of myself."

"Yeah, obviously, but it doesn't mean I can't help you out. You helped me."

"And it almost got me killed. Twice."

He smirks as he looks at the knife still at the ready in my hand. "Are you going to kill me if I try to help you? Even the score?"

I sheath my knife and take a step back, pressing my back against the cold, stone wall behind me. "I don't need your help. Thanks."

"Because you said 'thanks' and that probably nearly killed you, I'll let it go. But if you ever need anything will you ask me?"

"Probably not."

He grins. "You're difficult."

"You're dangerous," I mutter before I can think.

He lifts his eyebrows in surprise. He takes a step toward me. It's not much, he's not touching me, but I still feel claustrophobic because of it. Because of one small step.

"You scared of me, Joss?"

I snort. "What's there to be scared of?"

"That's not an answer."

"It's a dumb question."

"I don't think so."

He takes another step toward me.

"You don't think at all," I tell him, trying to sound angry but it comes out breathy and strained.

"I'm thinking pretty hard right now," he says, taking another step closer until he's nearly touching me. He's looking down at me with his warm eyes and I can see hunger in them. Not the Risen hunger I'm used to and not the starved animal hunger I see all around me during the winter. This is different. New. Exciting.

"You're thinking with the wrong parts," I whisper. "That's what makes you dangerous."

When he chuckles I feel his breath on my face. He doesn't back up and I don't push him away. I should. I should get out of here, away from him and never write on that wall again. But it's already been done and whatever damage we'll incur for all of this is already here or swiftly on the way. There are things I've seen, heard, felt and want that I never understood could actually exist outside the frame of my tiny TV. And this Pandora's Box, once opened, does not close easily.

I close the distance between us. I step up on my toes. I lean forward. I grasp his face in my hands and pull him closer.

I kiss him.

It's better than before. It's slower, easier. He holds on to me loosely, wrapping his arms around my waist and pulling my hips against his. His hands are big on my back, his breath warm on my face. I've never been held like this. I've never had hands touch me with such tense tenderness. I can feel the want coiled in them, the desire to push and gain whatever ground they can, but they hold off. He holds off. Ryan takes his time and reins them in, telling them to wait and there's a sweetness to that restraint that stands apart from all of the grappling, needy, violence of the world. It's such a contrast it makes my breath hitch in my lungs and my blood warm to the surface. I know I'm blushing as he kisses me. As he smiles against my mouth and I smile back and I think I laugh in the back of my throat. Or was it him? Either way, it's there between us and it's decadent and delicious.

He moves his mouth from mine. He trails it across my jaw, down under my earlobe and against my neck.

"You are," he murmurs, "the most beautiful girl I've ever seen."

I chuckle. "I'm probably the only girl you've ever seen."

He pulls his face back to look at me. "I've seen other girls. I wasn't born to this anymore than you were."

"You're right. I'm the only girl you've seen lately."

He lowers his eyes, shakes his head slightly. "That's not true either."

"Where have you seen other women?" He doesn't answer me. He keeps his arms around me and his gaze down, looking somewhere along my collarbone. Finally I ask, "Other gangs?"

He nods minutely as he meets my eyes again. His are apologetic and I'm instantly nervous.

"*Your* gang?" I ask, pushing away from him.

"No," he says firmly. "We don't keep slaves. Men or women."

"That's very noble," I say sarcastically.

Ryan scowls at me. His voice grows hard. "It kind of is. Even the Colonists are using people as slaves. Almost every gang in the city keeps at least a female or two. They bring them to market with pop up tents and use them as currency, a currency we don't take."

I look at him skeptically. "None of you?"

He grinds his teeth together briefly, his eyes angry. "Sometimes some of the guys will trade personal wares for time with the women. As a whole we don't do it but individually, well, that's their business."

"It's sick."

"I know."

"Have you ever done it?"

"I just agreed that it's sick," he says, sounding exasperated.

"Just because it's sick doesn't mean you won't do it. You didn't like killing a man but you did it anyway."

It's a low blow. Before the words are even out of my mouth I wish I could pull them back in.

His eyes are on fire now. "That's what you think? That's how you see me?"

I regret this conversation so much. How did we go from that kiss to this? How does this world seep into everything and rot it from the inside out? You can't find something beautiful here without it dying in your hand before you can make it home.

"You know what?" Ryan says angrily. "I'm out of here. Good luck."

He goes to step past me and into the light. Into the outside and out of my life and the pang in my chest is a gnawing pain that rips me wide open. How hard is it really? How difficult is it to have something and not throw it away because it's nothing like what you're used to? Nothing you've ever needed or had before. How hard is it to let yourself want something simply for the sake of wanting it? Just to make it yours?

My hand shoots out. I take his arm firmly. I meet his eyes, absorbing the anger rightly seated there and letting it burn into me. I let it teach me a lesson as it aches. I let it school me in never throwing a punch I don't care to see land.

"I'm sorry," I choke out. "I was wrong."

I don't know which of us is more shocked to hear it.

Chapter Ten

Ryan wants to start meeting on the regular. He asks if I'll meet him in the woods in the clearing where they killed the buck, but the memory of how deftly they cornered that animal and slit its throat open on the forest floor gives me pause. Years of conditioning scream at me, and even though I want to meet with him, I can't do it. I can't completely shake the idea that he's bait on a lure and I'm falling for it hook, line and sinker. He's disappointed when I tell him no. He's also a little annoyed because he knows *why* I'm saying no, but he accepts it. I'm skittish and I have every reason to be so this I do not apologize for.

He kisses me goodbye when he goes. It's short and sweet, full of promise. It's a lot of things I don't understand, things that scare the crap out of me, but it's also nice. Knowing he's out there and that he knows about me, thinks about me, is insane to me. It's like being split in half and existing in two places at once. It's disorienting. It's also exciting. I'm here in my home high up above the streets, but I'm also out there with him in the wild running with the Lost Boys across the crooked asphalt. He takes me places I could never normally go. He makes me free. I feel like I'm so much more than I used to be, taking up so much more space than I thought I deserved.

I'm present and so full. Like hidden music on a rooftop.

So of course I'm happy. I'm alive and happy and awake. Blindingly awake for the first time, and when I see a message on the wall a week later, I'm smiling when I answer.

Mornin', Beautiful.
I miss you.
How are you?

I'm waking up.

"It is pretty early."

I spin around, my hand going to my ASP, but I'm too late. The man behind me slams me into the wall, pressing my back hard against it until I feel like crying out in pain as the rough edges dig into my skin through the thin material of my jacket. But I don't. I don't cry and I don't scream. I take deep, calming breathes and I assess my situation.

It sucks.

The guy walked up behind me from down the street where I can see the silent rolling Colonist vehicles parked in the middle of the road. There are two of them, one with its back doors wide open and the other locked up tight. I count at least four other Colonists milling around the street, poking their heads inside buildings. They're looking for others that must be with me because I couldn't possibly have been alone. How would I have ever survived on my own?

"Where are—ooh!"

The guy doubles over in pain as my knee connects with his crotch, hitting him where it hurts. It's a dirty shot but do you see any refs out here? All's fair in the apocalypse. He lets go of me momentarily but that moment is all I need. I run from him as fast as I can, whipping out my ASP as I go. I leave my knife hidden against my jeans and under my jacket because if they do manage to get ahold of me, I want to have a surprise up my sleeve.

The Colonist's cry grabs the attention of the others and two come running at me. They're all men which pisses me off. No women in the roundup teams? What are they all doing? Sitting back at the Colony knitting winter sweaters, raising the children and making the meals. Sexist!

I swing the ASP and crack it down on the wrist of a man reaching out for me. It breaks it easily and he cries out louder than Crotch Shot back at the wall. I sprint for a small alley just across the street, hoping I can make it in and up the fire escape before they can get me. If I can do that, they'll never catch me. I know how to jump between the buildings from here for ten blocks easy. It's not something you do if you don't have to and certainly not something you try if you haven't practiced. They won't follow me, I know it.

I'm heading into the alley when a hand grips the back of my jacket and yanks me off my feet. My attacker easily lifts me up, then slams me down on the ground face first. I have to throw up my hands to keep from breaking my nose on the asphalt and my ASP flies away from me, skittering through the darkness into a pile of dirt and rubble. I'd have to search to find it and time is not a luxury I have anymore.

"Are you gonna be good?" the guy asks, breathing heavily. He barely ran. Boy needs more cardio in his life. It gives me hope that if I can slip away from him I can make it out of here. "Are you going to get up and go quietly?"

"Rick, you got her?" someone calls from down the street.

"What do you think, kitten? Do I got you?"

"Yeah," I say, feeling my knife's sheath digging into my hip bone "You got me."

"That's a good kitten," he grunts.

I'm pulled up onto my feet. He pushes me in front of him, still holding onto my jacket. Perfect.

"Let's go."

"Okay," I agree meekly.

I grab the zipper on my jacket, pulling it down hard and fast. The second it releases at the bottom, I throw my arms back, shrugging easily out of it and out of his hold. He gives a shout of surprise and frustration, but I don't care a thing for him. I'm running again. Unfortunately I'm running in the wrong direction. He had me pointed toward the vans. To my right is the wall but there's also Crotch Shot and he's recovered somewhat, vengeance heavy in his eyes. I can't get to the alley and open road behind Rick. I'm free but not for long. Not long enough. It doesn't surprise me that when I make a break for it past the vans, I'm clotheslined. I'm slammed back onto the pavement, the wind rushing out of my lungs and my head connecting sharply with the ground. I see stars as I struggle to keep conscious and drag air into my lungs. Neither comes easy. Hands lift me up and stand me on my feet. I sway, nearly toppling over, but a surprisingly gentle hand helps me stay steady. Another prods the back of my head and I flinch when I feel a sting.

"Get her inside, now!" a voice beside me shouts. "She's bleeding. It'll call the Risen straight to us. Let's move!"

I'm being pulled toward the back of the van and the gentle hand is starting to irritate me. I pull against it but it latches down harder, forcing me forward.

"You don't want to be out here dizzy and disoriented when the Risen show," the guy says calmly, sounding unreasonably reasonable.

"And unarmed," Rick says from behind me. I recognize his voice, his smug tone. I also recognize his hand on my butt as he shoves me toward the van.

"Not unarmed," I murmur.

I gather every ounce of clarity I can find inside myself and unsheathe my knife. I turn quickly, bringing up my hand as though I'm going to slap him. He grabs it easily, laughing in my face at my feeble attempt.

"Kitten has claws," he chuckles.

I sink my knife into his thigh. He was too distracted with my hand and deflecting the slap, he never saw it coming. His eyes say as much as the pain registers. While he's distracted by the knife in his leg, I thrust my head forward and up, straight into his nose. It breaks and bleeds into my hair, but I don't care. His shocked, bloody, broken face is worth it.

"You bitch!" he exclaims as he inhales sharply.

I'm tossed into the back of the van carelessly. The last thing I see before they close the doors isn't Rick's mangled face. It's not the concerned face of the guy with the gentle hands who sorrowfully tells me I shouldn't have done that. What I see far off in the distance, up high at the top of a building, is a flash of reflected light. Small and precise, like the mirror in a woman's makeup case. It casts a beam of light directly down on my face, making me wince. Then the doors slam shut and it's gone.

I'm gone.

***

"Are you cold?" a woman asks me.

I pull myself up off the freezing metal floor of the van, fighting against the rocking as it bumps silently down the uneven streets. I thought the back of the van was empty but it's not. There are three people huddled deep in the back; one man in his late twenties with two women. One is only a couple years older than I am while the other is easily older than the man. They're all bundled up tight, ready for the cold weather, and the man sits between them. Each of the women has her arms wrapped around one of his biceps, pulling him close.

"Um," I try to speak but my tongue feels thick. My head wobbles on my shoulders while the world tilts precariously.

"Uh oh," the guy says, rushing toward me. "She's going over. Nats, give her the sweater under your coat."

He has my shoulders firmly between his, holding me up as he looks me squarely in the face. I'm struck by how handsome he is. Dark hair, bright green eyes, chiseled features. The women look nothing like him, not even the same nationality, and I wonder how they all know each other. Just another band of survivors hiding out together?

Then it hits me through the fog. The way they were sitting together. The way Nats immediately jumped to it when he told her to give up her sweater, despite the cold. The angry hornet tattoo on his neck.

"You're in The Hive," I mutter.

"You've heard of us?" he asks absently, pulling the sweater over my head.

"No one in the wild hasn't heard of The Hive."

He shrugs. "I guess we're pretty well known."

"Well known?" I ask, pulling out of his grasp to finish dressing on my own. Pride and bravado, remember? Cornerstones of life. "Notorious is more like it. Feared is even better."

He sits back on his heels to give me an appraising look. His face is hard but I can see it is in his eyes. He's amused.

"You don't seem too scared right now."

I snort. "Not of you. You're not my biggest problem at the moment. Hell, you're not even my smallest problem."

He grins as he shakes his head. "What crew has been hiding you?"

"None. I'm not in one. Never have been." I look at him pointedly. "I never will be."

He laughs. "No joke? You've been going it alone?"

I nod, feeling ridiculously proud under his appreciative stare. "Six years now."

"That was a good run."

I move to sit at the end of the van with my back against the closed doors, the borrowed sweater pulled around me tightly.

"It's not over yet."

"Oh, *Kitten*," he says, emphasizing the word to

prove his point that they have me, "you know where you are. It's over."

"Don't call me kitten and it's not over until I'm dead."

The grin is wiped off his face as he watches me. I look back unsure but unflinching. Finally he heads back to his girls and I think I hear him mutter, "Where have you been hiding?"

We ride in silence for what feels like hours. I can't stand not being able to see outside. I can't tell what time of day it is. The rhythm of the jostling van is a problem for me too. It keeps lulling me to sleep and every time I nod off, I get yelled at.

"Wake up!" the hornet shouts, shattering the quiet.

I jerk my head up, startled awake for the fiftieth time.

"Quit yelling at me," I grumble, rubbing my temples. I have a killer headache.

"Quit falling asleep. You have a concussion. You'll die if you sleep."

I glare at him. "You know an awful lot. Taken a few hits to the head, have you?"

He ignores me. "What's your name?"

I eye him across the space between us, not sure how I want to respond.

He sighs impatiently. "Do I look like Rumplestiltskin?"

"What?"

"I'm not Rumplestiltskin. Giving me your name doesn't give me power."

"That's not how it goes," Nats chimes in. She's huddled in the corner beside the guy, the other girl asleep with her head in Nats' lap.

Her pimp frowns at her. "Are you sure?"

"Yep."

"I thought the whole point was a name exchange."

She nods. "It is, but it's the other way around. It doesn't make sense the way you said it. If she's hiding her name then s*he* would be Rumplestiltskin."

"Who would I be?"

Nats smirks. "You're a Queen."

He chuckles and turns back to me. "What's your name?"

"Joss," I reply warily.

I'm confused by the dynamic between Nats and the guy. It's not what I expected between a pimp and a slave. They almost seem like friends.

"Well, Joss, this is Natalie or Nats," the guy says pointing at the woman in the corner. "Snoring in her lap is Breanne."

"And who are you?"

Nats laughs. "He's a Stable Boy."

He looks at her indignantly. "I am *the* Stable Boy."

"What does that mean?" I ask, scared I already know the answer.

"It means he watches out for The Hive's women. Breanne and I included."

"Did a piss poor job of it today," he grumbles, fisting his hand and glaring down at it. I notice the cuts along the back of it, all of them fresh and enflamed. He threw some punches recently.

"Knock it off, Vin," Nats tells him harshly. He looks over at her, his face dark. "You did all you could for us."

"Then why are you in this van?"

"What's important is that we're not alone in this van. You could have left us, but you didn't."

"That's not a victory. I should have saved you."

"You're here, aren't you? Maybe you still will."

Vin chuckles darkly as he looks at his hands again. There's a dark metal ring on his left hand that he spins thoughtfully. Just as I'm about to doze off again he looks up at me, studying me. "Maybe Kitten here will help me."

"You saw what happened to the last guy who called me that, right?"

The smile Vin gives me then can only be described with one word; sexy. It's not something I'm terribly familiar with, but he wears it well.

"Help you do what?" I ask.

"Escape the Colony."

I take a deep breath, trying to focus on not falling asleep. It's becoming a struggle. My head aches so bad, I'd love nothing more than to lie down. "We haven't even gotten there yet. How do you know you won't love it?"

"Because I belong in the wild. So do you."

"You don't know me."

"I know a wild thing when I see it and you, Kitten, are a wild thing. Six years on your own? You don't want to be locked up in a cage or you would have joined willingly years ago. I'm still trying to sort out how you hid from the gangs all these years, let alone the Colonists and Risen."

"I found ways. You said it yourself, I don't want to be locked up in a cage."

"Or a stable?" Nats asks wryly.

I glance at her, not sure if I've offended her, but her face is placid.

"Not anywhere by anyone."

She nods in understanding but says nothing else.

Vin falls silent as well and soon the only sound in the van is Breanne's snoring along with the bump of the suspension on the rough, ruined roads. I doze off eventually. Vin lets me do it. Maybe he's got other stuff on his mind. Maybe he figures I'm not in his stable, I'm not his problem. I don't know how long I'm out but I wake with a start when the van slams to a halt.

"Get back here against this wall," Vin says urgently.

I scurry across the floor of the van to the back where I squat down next to Breanne. She's groggily sitting up, rubbing her eyes and looking more afraid with each passing second. She's the younger of the two women though she's still older than I am, but something in her face is almost childlike.

"So what do you say?" Vin asks me quietly.

There's a screeching of metal against metal, then a long yawning sound. We move forward again and the acoustics outside the vehicle change drastically. There's an echo. We must have entered some kind of building.

"You gonna help me get us out of here?" he asks.

The yawning again, then a deafening slam. All light coming in from any cracks in the door is extinguished and we're plunged in total darkness. I hear Breanne whimper pitifully.

"No one's ever escaped the Colonies," I whisper, feeling my heart leap into my throat as the silence drags out.

When Vin looks over at me the pull of his electric green eyes forces me to look back. He grins, his face fierce.

"There's a first time for everything." He reaches

out his hand, offering it to shake. To make a deal.

There's a screech of metal again, then another yawn, this time from the front of the van. We lurch forward. We're passing through something. We're entering their compound. This is real.

I hesitate only a moment before slipping my hand into his. I'm surprised to feel cold metal pressed between our palms and when I take my hand away I see that he's slipped a small, sharpened scrap of metal into it. It's not much, not even enough to call a knife. It won't kill but it will hurt.

"They're going to separate me from you girls," Vin tells me hurriedly as we roll quickly over surprising smooth ground. "Keep them safe and I'll work on our escape. Deal?"

The van stops. Doors are opened and slammed. Footsteps approach from both sides to meet at the back door.

"Do we have a deal?" Vin demands.

The door flies open. Bright afternoon light spills in, blinding us all. I hear footsteps thunder across the metal floor, then harsh hands lift me up and pull me away. Breanne screams. I hear Vin's deep, calm voice telling her to cool it. That it'll be alright. More feet, more hands, then cold air.

"Kitten!" Vin calls. I can hear him struggling in the back of the van. "Do we have a deal?!"

"Couple hours with her and you're already trying to pimp her?" a guy asks from beside me. "We don't play that way here. You're out of a job, buddy."

I've never made a deal with a Lost Boy before, certainly not a member of The Hive. I don't know that it's a smart thing to do. Saving Ryan has caused me a world of trouble. It's a mistake I really shouldn't repeat. It'll be easier to sneak myself out alone than try to get Vin, Breanne and Nats out with me. As far as anyone knows, no one has ever escaped the Colonies before. But maybe that's not entirely true. Maybe people like me have. Loners who found a way and slipped back into the wild with no one to tell the tale to. No one to welcome us home. No one to care if we lived or died.

"Joss!"

"Yes!" I shout back, surprising myself. My eyes are evening out, becoming adjusted to the light. I can see Vin's face now. He's being hauled out by three guys but he's staring straight at me, his eyes focused hard on mine.

"Yeah, Vin," I repeat calmly, slipping the shiv up into my sleeve as I step closer to his girls. "We have a deal."

Chapter Eleven

I have no idea where we are other than beside the water. In front of us is a huge white building with faded blue trim. It looks like a warehouse that was once dressed up to serve a grander purpose. Kind of like a train station or library. It squats on the upper left corner of a large lot full of green space that is being used for planting. The even rows suggest fields, though any crop is far out of season at the moment. I shiver against the cold, missing my jacket and hating being this close to the water. It surrounds the lot on all sides but one; the south side where we entered. When I look back at it I can see a row of multicolored, weathered shipping containers stacked two high. The line of them runs from shore to shore. Most containers are lined up end to end except for two right in the middle. They're running the opposite direction so that they can be opened and vehicles, like ours, are allowed to pass through. Now they stand locked up tight, an impassible barrier for zombies and Lost Boys. And us.

They take Vin away immediately, leading him through a side door and out of sight. He goes quietly once I've made my promise, but I can see the tension in his shoulders. The tightness in his step. They'd be wise to keep an eye on him.

Breanne, Nats and I are left standing out in the cold surrounded by three men on guard. I don't know what month it is but judging by the briskness in the air, I'd say it's almost December.

Christmas time.

The thought pisses me off almost more than being taken prisoner. Almost.

"Can we go inside yet?" Nats asks a guard, glaring at him. "It's kind of cold out here."

The guy with the gentle hands shakes his head apologetically. "We have to wait for the women to come get you. They'll take you to the showers."

"Hot showers?" Breanne asks hopefully. She's clinging to Nats' arm the way she was clinging to Vin before and I find myself getting annoyed with her. It'd be brilliant if it was all an act, making herself look meek and afraid only to throw them off, but I'm pretty sure this is her 100%. I'm already regretting taking on the role of babysitter.

"Hot showers," gentle guy says with a small smile.

"What then?" I ask, my voice hard. "What do you do with us then?"

"Then we'll get you something to eat." He smiles at Breanne again. "Something hot. After that you'll get a tour and you'll be assigned a bed. Then we'll help you get acclimated, start helping you find the right job."

"What if I don't want a job?"

His smile fades. "We all work. You'll need to contribute to stay here."

"I don't want to stay here. I don't want to contribute. So if you'll just show me the door…"

"You'll learn."

"Learn what? To like prison? No, thank you."

"This is for your own good," another guy tells me, his eyes pitying. "You can't survive out there alone. We're here to save you."

I glare at him. "I've survived out there alone for the better part of a decade. I don't need you or your protection."

He shakes his head sadly. "You'll learn."

I'm certain I don't want to know what they plan to teach me here.

A door swings open on creaking hinges, drawing all of our stares. Three women come out one by one in a line, all of them perfectly clean and groomed. Their soft, shining hair catches the sunlight and a small breeze, rippling like silk. They all look to be about late 20s or early 30s and they're all beautiful. I feel especially grimy just looking at them and I realize that with the chill in the air lately I haven't risked a full washing in almost a month. It's too cold to have wet hair this time of year.

A blond walks up to us, smiling brightly as she fakes a shiver. "Ooh, it's cold out, isn't it? Let's make this quick! Ladies and—oh, I thought we had ourselves a gentleman as well?" she says, looking questioningly at the men guarding us.

"He's already been taken in."

She blinks once long and hard but her smile never fails. It's the creepiest thing I've ever seen and, as you can imagine, I've seen some seriously creepy things in my day.

"No matter. At any rate, ladies, welcome to the MOHAI!"

We all stare at her blankly.

"As you may not know," she continues happily,

"the MOHAI was, and some of us feel still *is*, the Seattle Museum of History and Industry. It's a beautiful building with very exciting exhibits inside. Now, admittedly, we've taken a lot of them down and disposed of them due to space issues but there's still some fun stuff to see."

I look sideways at Nats. I'm relieved to see my confusion mirrored on her face.

What the hell is happening here?

"Now," says Tour Guide Barbie, turning serious, "we are so excited to have you here and we can't wait to show you just everything, but first things first. We have to get you cleaned up. So, if you'll follow me I'll take you straight to the showers."

As she turns her back, I look her and the other women up and down, searching for weapons. The men who have been standing guard all have utility belts on with knives, sharp screwdrivers and either a hammer or a heavy wrench. One even looks like he might have a Taser, something I've been eyeing since we left the van.

But the women appear to be defenseless. It has me thinking of the shiv in my pocket. As we follow them inside the door I note how they break us up. They usher in Breanne, then one of them, then Nats, another of them, then the blond ushers me in ahead of her with that saccharine smile of hers. If I get a chance to cut anybody today, it's going to be her.

The inside is warm and dry. And lit! There are actual light bulbs in sockets hanging from the ceiling at regular intervals. We walk down a long, narrow hallway that expands into a big open room, one wall of which is lined with showerheads. It's been stripped down to just cement walls and floors with a big drain in the middle and I wonder what it was before. Storage? A break room?

"Alright," the blond says, clapping her hands together sharply. The snap of skin against skin echoes through the large room sounding like a gunshot. "My name is Caroline. This is Melissa and Andrea. What we're going to do is get you clean. All of you. Every last inch. You've been living in the wild for so long we have to take some precautions, so this is going to be thorough. Please don't be embarrassed, we've all gone through it."

"What exactly are you going to do?" Nats asks, stepping closer to Breanne.

One of the other women, a brunette who I believe is Melissa, smiles at her reassuringly. "Nothing scary, don't worry. We're going to help you wash your hair with lice shampoo, use some exfoliating scrubs, use an antibacterial soap to eliminate… well."

"Bacteria?" I ask dryly.

She looks at me, her smile slipping. "Everything undesirable."

"So to begin, we need you all to strip down, please." Caroline says, closing the door to the hall and flipping the lock.

"Already locking us in?" I ask her.

"No, I'm locking the men out. Prying eyes are not welcome here. We want you to feel safe. Comfortable." She smiles broadly, catching eyes with Breanne. "Pampered even."

Breanne smiles as she begins to pull her clothes off. They look clean but worn out, something unavoidable on the outside, even in the stables of the biggest gang in Seattle. Nats joins her, though she does it with much less excitement. The shiny trio smiles approvingly at them then casts their eyes on me. I can't exactly escape right now, with or without Vin and the girls, and I'll be honest, a hot shower with real soap sounds amazing. But I'm worried about my shiv. I'm going to lose it, there's no two ways about that. I can't hide it from them here and I know they'll burn my clothes once I give them up.

Not wanting to be caught with it since that will put me under heavier watch, I walk to a bin in the corner. It's full of towels of all different colors, all folded neatly in stacks. I give the pretense of leaning against it to untie my shoe and deftly slip the shiv out of my sleeve. I let it fall inside the bin where it disappears in between the stacks of colorful cotton. I can't help but frown as I watch it go. That's three weapons I've lost today.

These women are thorough. Disturbingly, latex glove type of thorough. I feel a little violated after my shower. But I am clean. Really and truly clean for the first time in years. Putting on clean clothes (clean underwear!) feels amazing. When I run my fingers through my long, newly conditioned hair, it feels like cold satin against my skin.

They take us out of the washroom into another long hallway. It's cold in here and my wet hair chills me to the bone. It's then that I realize they've given us nothing substantial to wear. Nothing to keep warm in the outside for too long. Long enough to, oh I don't know, jump in the water and swim away? Once I hit that icy water, even if I made it to another shore without them catching me, I'd be frozen before I'd make it anywhere safe. That's not an accident on their part.

We enter into a large room with glittering silver

floors, wire mesh hanging from the ceiling and stark white plastic tables with matching chairs. There's a counter to the side made of worn old wood topped jarringly with sleek metal. The sterile beauty of it gives me whiplash and I take a step back, unable and unwilling to enter. I'm amazed at how well preserved this all is. When I catch a whiff of fresh baked bread, I regain the step I lost and then some. It calls to me, pulling me forward like a Siren ready to dash me on the rocks.

What reins me in is the fact that this room is bustling with people, all of them shiny and happy. All different ages, races, all clean, well fed, well maintained. And there are just so, so many of them.

"Vin!" Breanne shouts as she takes off running.

I spot him when she jumps into his arms like a girl in love. He hugs her loosely, nods at Nats and grins at me.

"You girls clean up well," he says, still looking at me.

"So do you. I don't think I've ever seen your hair that short," Nats tells him.

They've buzzed his hair until it's nearly gone. It's just a hint of darkness on his head, making his eyes seem brighter and his face look younger. He runs his hand over it, testing it out as he smiles ruefully at Nats.

"They have barber's sheers and I haven't had a real haircut in years. Figured why not." He glances at me. "What do you think, Kitten? Does it suit me?"

"I lost my shiv," I say, ignoring his question.

"Yeah, me too," he mutters, glancing at our escorts as they approach slowly.

Caroline smiles at him happily, taking all of him in. "I'm glad you found each other again. Excellent.

Why don't you all get in line, eat some lunch and then we'll give you the tour."

"Sounds great, thank you," Vin replies, smiling back at her.

She casts us each another glance then she and her minions shove off. When I look back at Vin, his smile is gone.

"I don't like her either," I tell him.

He nods. "She's trouble. Watch out for her."

"Can we eat now?" Breanne asks eagerly.

"Yeah, Bree. Go ahead. I'm right behind ya," Vin tells her, still watching Blondie as she walks away.

Getting food should be easy and fun. Walking up to a counter to pick what I want from where it sits warm and waiting for me sounds like paradise. But I'm in Hell. There are so many people here, easily 20 just in this room, and my skin is crawling. It's loud, it's hot, it's too full. My breath starts coming in short, strained gasps. I worry I'll hyperventilate. I hang back as Nats and Vin follow Breanne to the buffet line. I'm hovering in the doorway, both loving and hating the open space at my back, when Vin notices I'm missing.

"You okay?" he calls, his brow pinched in concern.

"I'm fine," I say breathlessly, shaking my head.

He whispers something to Nats before leaving the line to approach me.

"What's wrong?"

"Nothing. It's…" I try to even my breathing but I can't make it happen. "There are too— too many people. It's overwh—whelming. They're so loud and what if… what if one gets bitten? We'll all die. There are just too many!"

"Whoa, slow down," he says calmly, stepping into

my space and making me look at him. His face blocks out most of the room as he backs me against the wall. It's still loud and he's crowding me, but it's only one person. After Ryan I can handle it. This I'm better with. "Breathe slowly and deeply. Don't worry. Risen aren't getting in here. That's not what you need to worry about."

"They're always what I need to worry about," I mumble, feeling faint. "Them and you."

"Me as in gangs?"

"You as in ev—everyone else on the planet. Gangs, Colonists, d—dead, undead."

He pauses, chewing on that for a minute. When he speaks his voice is hard. "How big of a problem is this going to be?"

I lift my head, blinking up at him. "What?"

"Can I count on you or is this fear going to make you useless?"

I shove him away from me. It's a weak effort but he lets me do it. "It's not a fear, it's—screw you."

"No, you get it together. You're tougher than this, you have to be. No way you made it as long as you did alone if you can't adapt." He steps close again, his words rapid and low. "Those two girls I'm with, I can't count on them. Nats is solid but she's no fighter and Breanne is nothing but a pretty face. These people have taken a lot of guys from The Hive and I'm hoping to find some in here and get their help getting out, but who knows? Maybe they've gone native. Maybe they tried to escape and their dead."

"Maybe they were in the colony that fell."

He nods grimly. "Maybe. Right now you're my only sure thing. I watched you fight when they tried to take you. Even when they had you and you knew it, you didn't hesitate to put your knife in someone. So, please, tell me that girl is gonna be able to man up and handle this."

I glare at him, surprised to find myself breathing deeply. Evenly. Angrily.

"Can you handle it?" he presses.

"I can handle it," I growl.

He grins at my annoyance. "There it is, Kitten."

I make it through lunch because I have to. Vin doesn't say anything to Breanne or Nats about my problem but he sits us at a table on the outskirts of the room nearest the door. We eat in silence and though it's just bread, fruit and vegetables, it's delicious.

After lunch we get 'The Grand Tour' as Caroline laughingly calls it because she is just hilarious, and I find that the Colony is everything I dreamed it would be.

Absolute. Pure. Torture.

This building is huge and we don't even see all of it. Apparently a lot of it is used for 'storage', though storage of what we aren't told. We also aren't invited to ever find out. Most of the interior is broken up into work rooms, though quite a bit of it is sectioned off as living space. There are bathrooms, though not all of them work so you have to be careful, the showers, a common area that looks like it used to be an exhibit with a large TV and some seating, the kitchens beside the cafeteria and a large open area that was probably once the main exhibit but is now filled with beds. An old green airplane hangs high above in the ceiling, something I imagine could easily snap and crash down on unsuspecting sleepers, but what do I know? There's also a pink truck shaped like a foot. I don't ask. In fact, I don't ask anything. I don't say anything at all because with each step I take through this building, I panic a little more. People are everywhere, talking so loudly, constantly walking by, brushing past me, touching me to say hello as Caroline introduces us. I'm sweating rivers under the thin material of my prison clothes.

She shows us a large maintenance room where the electrical side of things is run and I finally get a reprieve from the crush of people. The generators are here, the solar batteries being charged by the panels on the roof and another set of batteries being charged by a small wind turbine set up outside in the yards. It all looks intricate and confusing to me but this is how they live. This is how they have hot running water, lights moderate heat and a functioning kitchen.

Outside is the small agricultural area we saw before. I also notice that they've taken the time to bring in high fences that run the three water sides of the property. No waiting for summer and swimming for freedom. How did they know? It's almost like they're as accustomed to keeping people in as they are to keeping zombies out. There are gardens and a greenhouse out here to be tended with small fruits and a lot of vegetables. There are also sections designated for various crops and they have livestock to be looked after; cows to be milked, eggs to be gathered.

Inside there are meals to be prepped, fruits and veggies to be canned and preserved, breads to be baked. The maintenance room needs bodies, the guards need people on rotation, there's sewing to be done. And that's all great. I'm actually in love with and on board for all of that. But what makes me want to scream in this woman's fake Barbie face is that I don't want to live here. I'm a butcher, not a baker or a candlestick maker, which, by the way, was on the tour as well. This entire community thing is not for me. I get it now, what Vin said about me earlier; I'm a wild thing. I belong in the wild, in the woods, in the streets. In danger.

When they showed me the giant room full of beds, I almost vomited. I can't take this. It's too crowded, too closed in. It's too *clean*. Don't get me wrong, I like being clean. I loved that hot shower and I will happily drink their milk until I get sick and die, but my problem with a lot of this is that it's like they're playing at normal. They're trying to pretend that they can hide behind these concrete walls and the world outside isn't dead and rotting at their doorstep. Their backyard is flooded with sewage and their solution is to draw the blinds.

People like me and Vin and Ryan, we live out there in the ugly and we look it in the eye every single day. We're out there trying to reclaim what was lost while these people are hiding away, pulling us in and trying to make us part of the fantasy that all can be bright and beautiful again if we just close our eyes to everything that's real.

I can see it on Vin's face too. As we walk through the tour Breanne gets happier by the second. I watch as he distances himself from her. She's lost to this place and he knows it. And who knows? If I was doing what she was on the outside, then I might be quick to sign up too. I'm not judging her for wanting this. I'm not judging anyone who would. What I am judging is the way they go about it.

"I want to watch this place burn," I say to myself.

Vin chuckles softly beside me. "You and me both, sister."

"Is this like what you guys have at The Hive? Is

everyone sitting pretty these days but me?"

"No, not even close." He glances around the common room we're standing in, his eyes landing on the 50in TV and brightly colored bean bag chairs. "This is almost grotesque."

"It's messed up, right?" I ask, glad he sees it the way I do. "It feels obscene somehow."

"Kinda disrespectful."

"Exactly. They're delusional."

"This one especially," he mutters, gesturing to Caroline.

As though feeling his eyes on her, she turns to face us.

"Everything all right?" she asks sweetly, the hard set of her mouth not matching her tone.

Vin grins at her. It's the same one he gave me in the van; all sex and charm. "It's amazing."

"We were just talking about how nice it is to be warm and dry," I agree, smiling at her.

"Wonderful." She doesn't believe a word of it. "Well, that's the end of the tour. Let's move on to dinner, shall we? It'll be a great chance for you to meet new people."

We start to file out of the room, Breanne following the three pretties like a happy puppy, Nats following warily and Vin and I bringing up the rear.

"'New people'?" I whisper to him. "They're going to separate us again."

"You cold and wet a lot, Kitten?"

I frown at him, startled by the question. "What are you talking about?"

"Answer the question."

"I don't know. Yeah. Everyone is."

"No," he replies, his tone low. "Not everyone is.

Nats isn't. Breanne isn't. I'm not."

"You're in The Hive, that's completely different. That's practically a Colony."

He glares at me. "We're not the Colonies."

"You know what I mean. The size of your gang compared to the others is huge. You don't have to hide like a lot of us do. In fact, you pretty much advertise your location. We all know where you are but none of us are dumb enough to come at you. I can't light fires half the time because someone is bound to see the smoke, and in case you haven't noticed, this is the Pacific Northwest. It tends to rain a bit. So yeah, I'm cold and wet a lot."

He shakes his head, looking annoyed. "You should join The Hive. You're a beautiful girl. You're high currency." He looks me up and down, taking in every curve of my body. "You're a hundred dollar bill, Kitten. An item would have to be pretty rare for The Hive to be willing to burn a Benjamin like you."

I scowl at him. "Is that supposed to be flattering?"

"It's supposed to be honest. And it is. I'm not stroking your ego, I'm being real. You'd hardly have to work. You'd be a trophy piece more than anything else. You'd be warm and dry, better fed."

"Why is everyone trying to save me lately? Ryan, the Colonists, you. I can take care of myself just fine."

"Who's Ryan?"

"No one," I grumble.

Vin grins wickedly. He nudges my shoulder as we walk. "You got yourself a guy, Kitten?"

"No."

He watches me and waits.

"Maybe," I admit grudgingly. "I don't know. Kind of."

He shakes his head sadly. "Giving it away for free."

"You're warped."

"Is he an independent too?"

"No, he's got a crew."

"And they don't know about you, do they?"

I shake my head fiercely.

"What crew does he run with?"

"I don't actually know their name. I just know where they are."

"Really? Where are they?"

I give him a long, blank stare. What am I? New? Ryan didn't sell me out, I won't sell him out. I owe him that much.

Vin chuckles. I nearly stumble forward when he suddenly slings his arm around my shoulders, pulling me in close beside him.

"Good girl," he murmurs, giving me a squeeze.

Chapter Twelve

They keep us fat and happy for another two weeks. Every meal is delicious, hot and filling, every night is spent in a soft bed with a warm blanket, and we're allowed a hot shower once per week. It is Heaven and it is Hell.

I'm not doing well with all these people. I'm barely sleeping and Vin is sometimes all the company I can handle at meals. They tried to make it easier for me initially by putting me in outdoor jobs. First it was the greenhouse and the gardens where I learned to pull weeds and water plants. Not much is growing right now but they say we have to make sure we have seeds to plant for next year and prep the soil for the spring. There is still broccoli, kale and even a few hearty pumpkins that have outlasted the drop in temperature that are growing and need tending. Other than that, though, gardening is as boring as I've always imagined it. I 'accidentally' break two clay pots in the greenhouse and I'm promptly kicked out.

Now I'm on guard duty which is a good change but a total joke. I'm tied to a guy named Phil up here on top of the wall of shipping containers with no weapon and no real purpose. We start walking back and forth, he and I starting at one end, another guy at another end. I can see three more people walking the chain link fences surrounding the rest of the property, dutifully keeping the Kraken out. I asked why we needed fences against the water. Phil's response was priceless.

"For safety."

They never acknowledge that we're captives here. It's always 'Thank goodness we found you!' and 'You'll get used to it. You've been away too long." Away where? Out living my life on my own terms? They act like they're CPS and we're runaways or victims of Stockholm's Syndrome. They will heal us! It's unreal.

"Joss, you're looking the wrong way," Phil barks.

I look at him, confused. "How? I'm looking out there. I'm watching for... stuff."

"What stuff? What are you talking about?"

"Well, I assume I'm not watching for Risen because," I throw my arms wide across the city. This area is absolutely swarming with Risen. It's far worse out here than it is in my part of town. Their moaning is a constant hum in my ears up here. "There they are, pretty much everywhere. And we're not killing them, which is weird, but ok. So I'm watching for whatever else. Gangs, I guess?"

Phil shakes his head, ignoring my sarcasm. "No, you're watching the inner courtyard."

"Why? What's the threat there?"

"Look, the outside is fine. Just worry about what's going on inside."

I stop following him. "You mean we're not watching to keep anything out, we're making sure everyone stays in?"

"The people need to be kept safe."

"From what? The cows?"

"Themselves," he says firmly. "Now walk."

I follow him but I want to shove him off the structure. I daydream about it for the rest of my shift. Getting out of here was going to be tough but now that I've seen all of this, the Risen outside and the guards watching every corner, it feels impossible.

"That's why they showed it to you," Vin tells me.

We're standing in the back of the common room after dinner with some of the people in our rotation. The Colony is divided into three groups who live on three different schedules. It ensures that someone is awake, on watch and working at all times. It's like a 7-Eleven; it's always open.

"Well, it worked. I'm worried."

"Don't be. I'm working on something."

"Oh yeah? What?"

"That."

He nods in the direction of a group of women sitting on the floor across the room. They're watching a movie playing on the television, some bubble gum 90s romance monstrosity that makes me ache for the brilliance that is John Hughes, and I can see Barbie sitting in the center of it. Breanne is with her looking every bit the team player. I've already counted her as one of them.

"Breanne?" I ask incredulously. "What? Is she doing an inside job?"

I can't believe it could be true. Breanne is a sweet girl but she is simple. She would find the layers of an onion confusing.

"No, I am. On her." He points to my nemesis.

"Barbie?"

"Caroline."

"Whatever. How are you working an inside job on her?"

He looks at me pointedly but doesn't say a word. I stare back at him, not getting it, not until—

"Oh, God, gross."

He grins. "There it is."

"But you hate her."

"Violently, yeah. Girl's dead inside. But when a woman offers to get naked for you, you don't pass that up. Not in this economy."

"I would think in your line of work that you'd be at the point where a naked woman is not that exciting."

He snorts. "If I ever get to that point, I better be dead."

"So are you just sleeping with her or are you getting something out of her?"

"Oh, I get something out of her. Every time. I'm very thorough."

"Again, gross. Are you getting anything useful to the rest of us?"

"Not yet, but give me time. Right now she's slumming but once she starts falling in love with me she'll start spilling her secrets. Pillow talk is very important."

"Once she's in love with you? So this is a long con. The kind of plan that has no hope of getting off the ground before I'm old and gray like you."

"Ouch," he chuckles. "Do you have so little faith in my charms?"

I shrug, not looking at him. I have no doubt about his charms. In fact, if I was a ten years older...

"Not your type, huh? Not like your boy Ryan?"

"Don't talk about him," I say quietly.

"Why not?"

"I don't like to talk about him."

I don't like to think about him. Not in here. My memories of whatever it was we had, whatever was starting between us, are starting to fade and distort. He's on the outside living free and wild with the Lost Boys and the part of me that I imagined with him feels far and faint right now. As though it's ceasing to exist. As though maybe it never did.

"Will he look for you?" Vin asks softly, his usual careless bravado shelved for a brief moment.

I shrug, watching the screen fixedly. There's a guy talking to a girl on the busy streets of a large city. He reaches up to push a lock of her hair behind her ear. She beams up at him like an idiot. Like that small, simple gesture means the world to her.

"I doubt it."

"If he went missing would you look for him?"

Rain begins to fall. The guy pulls out an umbrella to cover her but she pushes it aside. They're drenched in an instant, both of them a mess. They kiss.

I feel the pang in my chest again.

I nod. "Yeah. Yeah, I would."

***

Two nights later I visit Nats at her newly assigned work station. She's in the maintenance room, the place that impresses and intimidates me most. I think it's because of the dull hum of electricity, something I've nearly forgotten about. That of all things feels the strangest to me. Functioning lights that go on and off with the flick of a switch. Power readily available at your fingertips whenever you need it. It was such a huge part of my life before the world ended, one I never actually thought about, and to have it back is almost unnerving. It's like an old friend you thought was long dead is back and insisting they're alive. I don't trust it.

Nats is thriving here in this room. She's working with just one other person on her shift. When I sit down across from her at the table where she works, I think I hear him snoring. His head is on his folded arms resting on a desk. He didn't move when I enter the room.

"Hey, how's it going?" I ask, perching in front of her.

"Good," she says distractedly, making notations on a chart and frowning.

"Something wrong?"

She purses her lips, then tosses the pen aside. "No, not really. I was just noticing how inefficiently they're using the power here. If they'd divert it from some sections to others at regular intervals, moving with the shifts, it would make so much more sense. They need to create dead zones, yanking the power entirely from areas like the dorms. Someone is always sleeping, why do you need power flowing there? If you need light, use candles. And the useless bathrooms. You can't flush the toilet but you can turn on the light. Why? It's ridiculous."

I lean forward to look at the chart in front of her. It's gibberish to me. Confusing, foreign language, Greek gibberish.

"You got that from looking at this chart?"

"Yeah, it's all here, plain as day but none of them want to see it," she grumbles.

I shake my head. "Scary as the thought may be,

I'm with them. You're a genius, Nats, cause this all means nothing to me."

"Just below, actually."

"What?"

"Just below a genius," she says casually. "At least by the standards set before. Now I'm considered a moron because I can't skin a cat and cook it for dinner."

I smile at her. "It's an acquired skill. What did you do for a living before the world fell apart?"

She shakes her head, standing up and gesturing for me to do the same. "That doesn't matter now, it's in the past."

I follow her as the takes up the clipboard and begins her rounds. "You don't like to think about it?"

"There's no sense in thinking about it."

"Ok," I say, dropping the topic. I don't like talking about life before either so fair enough.

She sniffs the air around me. "Do they have you in the kitchens now?"

"How'd you know?"

Nats smiles. "You smell good. Like pumpkins."

I nod. "I was canning. They do a lot of canning in there."

"Did you know how to do that before?"

"No," I scoff. "Do you know how?"

"Yep, but I'm from a different generation. Do you like it in the kitchen?"

I shrug as I step closer to one of the generators. There's a discoloration on the side like rust. I run my finger down it. "It's alright. Better than the gardens."

"But you don't like it?"

"I don't hate it."

She looks where I'm touching the generator and

frowns. "Make friends in there."

I straighten up, scowling at her. "Why?"

"Because something is rotten in the state of Denmark," she tells me, her voice dropping low. "I promise, you not everyone is happy to be here."

"Really?" I ask, shocked. They all seem so... brainwashed. "How do you know?"

She gestures silently over her shoulder toward the sleeping guy and mouths the words *Not happy.*

I look over my shoulder at her co-worker but he's still out cold. I turn to ask Nats who else isn't happy but I catch her frowning at the generator again.

"What's wrong with it?"

"I don't know," she mutters. She reaches out to touch the discoloration. "It looks like rust but I don't think it is. The pattern is all wrong."

"Could be blood," I say offhand.

She looks at me sharply. "Do you think it is?"

"I don't know. Looks like it. If it is, it's old."

"They said this facility wasn't that old. They haven't been here very long," she mutters to herself.

"This thing had to come from somewhere else. It was probably salvaged from an old building. Maybe the blood got on it there."

"Maybe," she says, still frowning.

There's a snort from the guy on the desk and Nats steps back, her entire demeanor changing. She's suddenly light and happy.

"Where's Vin tonight?" she asks loud and clear.

I roll my eyes. "With Caroline."

"He's working that angle hard, isn't he?" she asks, shaking her head.

"Does he really do it to get information out of her or is he doing it—"

"You mean doing her," Nats says with a smirk.

"Sick. Is he doing it just because he can? Or to show he can?"

"Oh, honey," she laughs, "he knows he can. Have you seen Vin? Just because you have your heart and panties all knotted up over some boy on the outside, it doesn't mean Vin isn't a show stopper."

"He told you about that?"

"He tells me about everything. And here's my take on what he's doing with Caroline. It's a power trip. He's spent his entire life, even his life before this one, under someone else's rule. Out there in the wild he can't do much about that. He's risen as high as he's gonna go and he knows it. But in here he has options. And I think that's what he's doing with Caroline. He's exerting power and control. He's in charge with her and he likes it. Sort of his way of literally stickin' it to the man."

"What was he before?" I ask, trying to shake away the imagery that phrase is attempting to force into my mind.

"He was you," she says, matter of fact. "And that's why he likes you so much."

"What do you mean he was me? Ten years ago nobody was living like I do."

"Vin was. He was a kid your age from the wrong side of town living almost exactly as you do now. A runaway alone, trying to avoid becoming affiliated with a gang and scraping out a life for himself. And he wanted more, just like you."

"I don't know that I've ever wanted more," I say softly, feeling embarrassed somehow. "I think I've always just wanted to keep what I had."

"This Ryan of yours, is he something new for

you?"

"Yeah," I admit softly.

"He's something different. Something more, and I can tell from your eyes that he's something you want. You're a hard as nails survivor and a closet softy. So was Vin. He still is, he's just locked up the softy in the closet tight and he'll never let him out again."

"It's probably for the best, right?"

She shrugs. "That's not my place to say. Everyone has to decide for themselves how they want to handle this life. You need to choose whether or not you want to survive or you want to live."

I stare at my hands thinking of brown eyes, stolen kisses, scribbled messages and how, despite my present situation, it was all worth it.

"Living is harder, isn't it?" I ask, looking up at her. "It's more dangerous."

"Much more," she agrees. Then she smiles at me. "Which is why I know you can do it."

***

That night I wake up to the blurry sight of a dark face coming at me. A hand grips my head, clamping down on my mouth. It's my worst nightmare come true; a crawler catching me sleeping.

I don't have time to think. I go on autopilot and my system is programmed for violence. I punch the face as hard as I can. There's a groan as I make contact and the hand falls away from my mouth. I sit up quickly, rear back and punch again, this time catching the thing in the side of the head behind the ear. It screams, something that should strike me as odd, but I ignore it. I'm still half asleep and scared out of my mind so it could stand up, plead for mercy forwards, backwards and in Latin and I'd still beat its face in.

I grab the pillow off my bed as I launch myself at the figure. I grab its dark hair and yank its head back hard until it falls backwards onto the ground. Then I pounce. I'm straddling its chest, just about to bring the pillow down over its mouth to protect me from its teeth while I drive me knee down on its throat until it snaps, when it speaks.

"Please don't! Please stop!"

I hesitate. My chest is heaving and every muscle in my body is screaming to finish the job, but I rein it in. I take in my surroundings. I remind myself where I am. Who I'm with. When I look down, I realize with horror that I'm about to kill a living human being.

I scurry backwards away from her until I'm pinned up against my bed's frame.

"What the hell?" I gasp.

The girl sits up slowly, swaying side to side. She's holding her hand to the side of her face where I punched her in the cheek. I can't see her very well in the dark, but I know that's going to bruise because my right hand is aching. It's nothing compared to what she must be feeling. Or what she'll be feeling tomorrow.

"What's going on?" someone calls from the other side of the room.

"Nothing," my assailant calls lightly, shaking her head like she's trying to clear it. I got her good behind the ear. Her equilibrium will be jacked for a while. "The new girl had a bad dream. I came over to check on her. She's fine."

"Go back to sleep," someone else grumbles nearby.

"We are," she replies. As she stands up, she has to

grab onto a nearby bed to keep her balance. She offers me her hand. "Right, Joss?"

I shake my head and stand up on my own, watching her closely. She's drenched in shadows and I can't make out her face. All I know is her height, build and that she'll have a hell of a black eye tomorrow.

"This isn't over," I whisper fiercely. "I'm gonna find you."

She nods faintly and whispers, "I hope you do."

Chapter Thirteen

The next morning I'm on shiner watch. I'm looking at every woman I pass trying to find long dark hair, a petite build and a face with my knuckles written all over it. At breakfast I sit with Vin as I always do, but I notice we're not alone. Two other men about his age come to sit with us and a middle aged woman I've never seen before sits herself right down beside me. I look her over quickly. Too tall.

"Joss, have you met Sandra?" Vin asks, gesturing with his fork between myself and the Amazonian beside me. I'm surprised by his genial tone and use of my actual name.

"No. Hi," I reply curtly.

Vin frowns at me but I ignore him. He talks and laughs with his new friends as I slowly eat my pancakes. Throughout the meal, I scan the crowd. I don't see anyone that fits the shadow I wrestled with last night and I'm starting to wonder if she's even on the same sleep cycle. Maybe she was just coming off shift when she decided to stop by and try to murder me.

As the room clears out I begin to lose hope of finding her today. Vin's friends eventually leave. I go to stand to leave as well but he stops me by slamming his hand down on my tray, knocking it back to the table loudly.

"What's your deal?" I exclaim, glaring at him.

"I was going to ask you the same thing."

"What are you talking about?"

"You need to get to making friends with these people."

I shake my head and look away. "You sound just like Nats."

"She's a smart woman, you should listen to her. I know social skills aren't your thing, but at least try."

"Why do we need to make friends with them?"

"To use them."

"That's chipper."

"Do you want out of here?"

"Yes."

"Then get off your high horse and help me out."

I sit back from him, taking in his angry eyes and the harsh line of his mouth. He's never been mad at me before. It's intimidating and I hate that he can do this to me.

"What are we using them for?"

"Eric and Tim, the guys sitting beside me who you ignored, they work in the fields. Do you know where the fields are?"

"Outside the building where we're not allowed," I reply quietly.

None of us were selected for outdoor duties permanently. Not yet. We've had private counseling sessions with our Team Leaders (mine is Melissa and I'm just grateful it's not Barbie) to discuss our transition into the community. Despite his charms, Vin wasn't chosen to go outside either. They don't trust us near the fence lines unsupervised. I can't say I blame them. Given the chance, I'd risk the freezing waters to get out of here. No question.

"And Sandra works in the laundry. How could the laundry be helpful to us, Joss?"

I thought it was weird that he was using my name before, but I find it condescending and annoying now. He's treating me like a child. I'm thinking I've already punched one person in the past 24 hours and I wouldn't mind doing it again.

"Clothing. Warm clothing and lots of it."

"Nailed it," he says, smacking his hand on the table loudly. "Next time I expect you to act a little friendlier and remember that we would like to get out of here before we die."

He rises to leave but I stand quickly as well, leaning over the table and shoving my finger in his face.

"And next time *you* try and remember that you're not my pimp, I'm not one of your girls and if you want my help, you'll watch the way you talk to me. Understood?"

This is a moment in my life when I seriously wonder if I'm going to get slapped. I'm mouthing off to a Stable Boy from The Hive, a guy whose job it is to keep women in line, doing what they're told and making the very testy, very violent men at the top of his food chain happy. He minds the coffers and the coins all have PMS. It can't be an easy job. It could easily be one he manages with an iron fist.

His jaw works under the taught skin of his face. It clenches and releases as he chews on what I've said. He carefully, dispassionately considers me. His calm is freaking me out. I'd rather he was yelling. I'd almost rather he hit me. Eventually what he does is smile.

"Understood, Kitten," he replies, his voice low and rough.

His eyes bore into me with a heat that I recognize. A hunger I've seen before. It reminds me of Ryan and it hurts in my heart like you wouldn't believe. I haven't let the thought sink in because it's massively inconvenient and wholly unlike me, but it's undeniable. I miss him.

I lower my hand. "Don't."

He grabs my hand before I can pull it back. He uses it to pull me forward over the table. I have to brace myself on my other hand so I don't fall over. Suddenly my face is inches from his.

"Don't what?"

I look him hard in the eye and shake my head firmly. "Don't make it like this. We're not like this, you and I."

"Who's to say we couldn't be?"

"Me."

He chuckles. It smells like honey, dripping and sweet. "Come on, Kitten. Don't you ever get tired of being alone?"

"Are you gonna fix that for me, Vin? Are you gonna be with me and stay with me forever? Can you handle that?"

"Is that what you're looking for?" he asks me, his voice and grip tightening. "The fairytale and forever after? Because I'll break it to you now; it's a myth. It always has been."

"I'm not holding out for forever. I'd be happy with tomorrow but you can't even promise me that, so let's stop this before it gets weird and we can't come back from it." I feel eyes on us and I look over his shoulder to see Caroline there in the doorway. Her eyes are livid. They're promising me the eternity Vin can't, only this one I imagine to be far less enjoyable. "And before your girlfriend gets the wrong idea."

"My what?" He follows my eyes over his shoulder. When he sees Caroline he curses, clenching his hand and pinching mine in the process. I let out a small whimper of pain that makes him jerk his head back to me. "What's wrong?"

"Let go of me," I say, swatting at him. When he releases me I rub my hand, trying to ease the ache.

"What happened to your hand?"

"I got in a fight," I grumble.

He raises an eyebrow in surprise. "Did you win?"

I glare at him. "Are you serious? Of course I won."

"What happened?"

"A girl jumped me while I was sleeping. I punched her in the face. Then in the ear. Finally she went away."

"Why?"

"Because I punched her," I enunciate slowly.

"Why did she jump you?" he growls.

"No idea," I say, looking back at the doorway. Caroline is gone. She's too short and the hair color is all wrong anyway. "But if it happens again, I'm finishing what she started."

***

Four days after the attack I still haven't found the girl who did it. I'm wondering if she's hiding and her words about wanting me to find her were all talk. I cross paths with Nats and ask her to keep a look out on her shift, but so far no luck there either. I'm beginning to think the chick is a magician and either escaped or has moved on to another Colony.

I take Nats and Vin's advice. I start to make friends with the people in the kitchen. There are six of us in there during our shift, four women and two men. I find it surprisingly easy to talk to them, almost like they were waiting for me to give them the chance. And what do they want to hear about most from the girl from the outside?

The gangs.

"Is it true they eat people?" Steven, a portly forty-ish guy asks me.

He's one of the very few people I've seen in the last decade with any kind of weight problem. I have a feeling it's got a lot to do with the 'tasting' that he does in here. He's the head chef and rightly so. The man is a wizard with water, carrots and thyme. I'm convinced he could make manure edible.

"Some of them do," I say cautiously, cutting up apples. Endless amounts of apples for canning and eating and applesauce and apple bread and who knows what else. "Not all of them, though. As far as I know, there's only one gang that does."

"Have you ever seen them?" Crystal asks. She's about Steven's age but whisper thin with hair almost as red as mine.

"Yeah, from afar. They look totally normal. Just like you and me," I tell her, heading off the question I see coming.

People think that just because you eat someone you look like a freak. Not so. Serial killers were charming, upstanding members of society back when there was one, and the cannibals in the wild are the same way. It's the freakiest thing about them; their normalcy.

"Do they really keep Risen as pets?"

"Not that I've ever seen, but I've heard about zombie fights."

"What, like boxing a zombie?" Steven asks, wrinkling his nose in disgust.

"No, like cock fights."

"Oh. How do you get them to fight each other?"

I don't answer. I don't want to, not around all this food. How they do it… it's disturbing. It involves masks. What the masks are made of is the key here. That is if it's true, which it might not be. I actually really hope it's not.

Amber, a brunette with bright eyes and a face that reminds me of Breanne, changes the subject. I'm eternally grateful.

"Is it true most guys in gangs are gay?"

I laugh so hard I almost cut my finger instead of the apple. Tears spring in my eyes. "Please ask Vin that. Please!"

Amber laughs as well, but blushes. She'll never ask him but I don't care. That moment in the kitchen is the best and brightest I've had in weeks. I feel like I'm doing Nats and Vin proud making friends. But for some reason Melissa pulls me out of the kitchen a few days later and gives me some terrible news.

It's time for me to try my hand at sewing.

I wish they'd let me save us all the trouble and listen to me when I say that this is not my place. But Melissa isn't hearing any of it.

"You'll do great!" she beams, leading me through the building to where they store the machines and fabrics. "Everyone has hidden talents. You have so much potential but you've been robbed of the chance to experience it. We're giving that back to you. It's so exciting!"

I am not excited.

She continues to lead me toward the sewing room, which I think is odd. I know where it is because I saw it on the tour. I tell her as much but, again, she isn't hearing it.

"I want to make sure you meet everyone and get settled in," she insists.

She wants to make sure I show up is what it is and fair enough. Left unattended, I wouldn't set foot in that room. As it turns out I'm glad I do. The second we walk in and all heads lift from their work to see who has arrived, I come face to face with my attacker.

The room is laid out long and narrow. A large loom that I imagine was part of an exhibit sits at the far end along with two ancient looking sewing machines, the kind from the old days that you pedaled with your feet instead of running on electricity. Most of the 10 or so women in here are sitting at long tables with baskets of fabric, pins, patterns and God knows what else in front of them, but I only have eyes for one.

"Everyone, we have a newbie here," Melissa sings, pulling me forward to put me on display. "This is Joss. She's been through a lot of the outdoor jobs recently, staying out in the fresh air. She's needed to take her time adjusting to the good life."

She smiles at me as the room breaks into small chuckles.

I smile faintly, trying to look sheepish. "I'm blown away by having a hairbrush again. Everything else is a little overwhelming."

More soft chuckles around the room. I can feel all

eyes on me as they weigh me down with their pity. Melissa even whispers an 'Oooh' and rubs her hand on my back. I resist the urge to shake free.

"Well, that nightmare is over. You're safe and sound with us now, sweetie. Girls, let's make her feel at home, alright? Who would like to show her the ropes?"

All hands in the room rise eagerly. All but one. I look at my attacker and watch as she tentatively raises her hand, obviously not sure about being in close quarters with me. But if she doesn't raise her hand like everyone else it will look suspicious. The sheep mentality of this joint rolls over me hard in a hot, smothering wave.

I have got to get out of here.

"Lovely, thank you!" Melissa cries, happy to see everyone so eager to take me on. She gestures to the group and smiles at me. "Take your pick."

I pick the hesitant girl with the fading yellow bruise around her eye.

She's about twenty five or so, petite and kind of mousy. I'm pretty surprised she felt confident enough to take me on. My left shoe weighs more than this girl.

She watches me closely as I walk toward her and sit down slowly at her end of the table. I'm sitting directly beside her specifically to make her nervous. I'm in her peripheral but there's nothing separating us, there are sharp scissors in her basket only a foot away from me and I'm a big angry unknown for her.

I smile warmly, extending my hand to her. "I'm Joss. What's your name?"

"Lexy," she murmurs.

"Not gonna shake my hand, Lexy?" She doesn't answer. "Probably smart. I have a pretty brutal handshake. Nice eye, by the way."

"Nice right hook," she replies, turning to look at me.

I smile again. "I have a lot of practice."

"That answers my question then."

"What question? Whether or not I can take you? Shouldn't have even been a question."

She shakes her head, looking away. "I wasn't looking for a fight."

"You grabbed my face in the dark while I slept. If not a fight, then what were you looking for?"

Lexy glances down the length of the table nervously. I look as well and catch all eyes on us. They quickly go back to their work.

"I was looking for you," Lexy whispers.

I frown. "Why?"

"There are rumors that one of you in the group that just arrived was living alone on the outside." She leans in closer to me. I think it's a brave move because I don't like it. At this point, even I don't know how I'm going to respond to her. "A lot of people think it was that girl Nats, but I've always thought it was you."

"Why does it matter?"

"Because you know stuff. Stuff that isn't filtered by the gangs or… other people," she replies as though it were obvious.

Now I'm intrigued. "What stuff am I supposed to know?"

"How's it going, girls?" Melissa asks, appearing out of nowhere.

"Great," Lexy says with a buoyant smile. She's good at turning on the happy, a lot like Vin, and I remind myself to be wary of her. "We were just talking. Getting to know each other. What pattern do you want me to teach her?"

"Something simple to start. I don't think she's going to be much of a seamstress, right, Joss?"

Her sweet tone makes my skin itch. Do they teach that tone here? The pitch of the voice that rides in your veins and vibrates at a frequency that makes you feel like you're ready, willing and able to murder puppies in front of children? What kind of jacked up witchcraft is that? It's like the devil's brown note.

"Dead friggin' on, Mel," I tell her happily. "I'm better at ripping things apart than putting them together."

Melissa smiles tightly as she retreats to the doorway. She stands watching the room but really she's watching me. I'm pretty sure that ripper comment is going to get back to Caroline which means it will probably get back to Vin and I'll get another lecture. Woo. Hoo.

"So this pattern is for a children's t-shirt. It's the easiest one we have," Lexy says, pulling out material and laying it in front of me.

"That's great," I say, pushing it aside. "What stuff do you think I know?"

"Nothing," she mutters, glancing at Melissa. "It's not a good time."

"You must have thought I knew something good if it was worth sneaking up on a girl from the wild while she was sleeping. So what was it?"

She doesn't answer me. I sigh. I'd rather she wanted a fight. This is annoying.

"Why are we making children's shirts?" I ask, examining it. There's a lot of letters and symbols all over this thing but none of it means anything to me. "I haven't seen a single kid here."

"Not in this Pod, but there are children in others. They grow so fast, go through clothing so quickly, we all help make things for them."

"That's what you guys call each other? Pods?"

"Yeah. What—" She takes a breath. "What do you call us on the outside?"

"Colonies," I say with distaste. "You're all the same thing to us."

"How many are there?" she asks, her voice barely audible.

"How many of what are there? What are you asking?"

"How many Pods? How many Colonies are there?"

"How should I know? Three I think, though probably more," I say, surprised by the question. "Wait, do you not know? How do you not know?"

Her eyes dart to Melissa as she fiddles with the pattern absently. "They don't tell us."

"That's weird."

"They don't tell us a lot of things."

That, I think, is not so weird. This Colony is smaller by far than the other two in the stadiums and I wonder if they're the only ones kept in the dark. Are there larger Colonies somewhere else that keep secrets from the stadiums?

"Did they tell you that the zombie population was almost gone a couple months ago?" I ask casually, taking a gamble.

She freezes, her brows pinching in confusion. "That's impossible. Have you seen how many Risen are outside?"

"Yeah and it's nuts compared to downtown. Up until recently, when one of your Pods fell, the Risen

163

weren't even much of a problem."

Lexy stares at me, her eyes suddenly sharp. "What makes you think a Pod fell recently? How recently?"

I study her face and I wonder how far I should go with this conversation. Twice now I've seen how quickly this girl can flip the switch and become someone else when the need is there. I wonder if I'm seeing the real her now or if this is all an act to draw me out. To find out what I know about their operation. Maybe she, Mel and Caroline are the best of friends and I'm sewing with the enemy here.

I push the pattern across the table toward her and sit back in my chair. "Why don't you go ahead and show me how to make that shirt now?"

***

Vin shakes his head. "That's not a shirt.

"It is too a shirt!" I cry indignantly. "Nats, tell him it's a shirt."

Nats, who is just waking up and enjoying a rare moment with us, sighs warily. "Honey, it's not even close."

"What? Yes, it is. It has a neck and sleeves. I worked really hard on this!"

"Put it on then," Vin challenges.

I scowl at him. "It's a child's shirt. I can't fit in it."

"Too many waffles."

"Excuse me?!"

He pulls the shirt from my hands and holds it up in front of me. "Show me where the kid's arms fit through."

I roll my eyes. "They fit through the sleeves, here

and her—ah hell."

I've sewn the sleeves shut.

"Do you see why it's not a shirt now?"

"Shut up," I mutter, snatching the shirt back from him.

Despite our awkward moment, Vin and I have fallen back into our regular routine. Caroline must have been thoroughly reassured of his affection for her (a thought that makes me ill) because she hasn't given me the murderous look she did in the cafeteria. She still hates me, that much is clear, but she looks at me more like she wants to end me quickly as opposed to dancing in my blood.

"So this girl that attacked you," Nats asks, thankfully changing the subject, "you couldn't get a read on her?"

"No, not really," I admit. "I mean, I think she's legit but then again people aren't really my thing, you know?"

"Yeah, we know," Vin says emphatically.

I throw the non-shirt at his face.

"How's Breanne doing?" Nats asks.

"She seems alright," Vin tells her gently. "Caroline's really taken her in."

"Caroline really *takes in* a lot of people," I say brightly. "Right, Vin?"

He smiles. "I knew it. I knew you were dirty. I just had to wait and have faith."

"So you think she's okay?" Nats presses.

"Yeah, I think she's great. Places like this, they really do work for some people. Breanne is one of them. She's happier here than she ever was at The Hive."

"And you're not worried about going back and

having to tell Marlow you lost a dime?"

"What's a dime?" I ask.

Vin looks at me pointedly. "You remember what I told you about currency?"

"Yeah."

"Breanne is a dime. A tenner."

"What, like ten dollars?"

"Yeah."

"Are you serious?!" I cry, feeling massively insulted on Breanne's behalf. "That's insane. She's beautiful."

"Not really," Nats says evenly. "She's pretty, sure, but that's not all that matters. Personality plays a big part and she's sweet, but she's not much else."

I want to ask Nats what she is. If she's a dime as well, though I can't believe she would be, not as smart as she is. But I'm worried it'd be offensive to ask. I'm also blown away by the fact that Vin labeled me a hundred dollar bill. What is it about me that sets me so high?

I look up to find him watching me, his eyes amused. He knows exactly what I'm thinking.

"You flattered yet, Kitten?"

I can feel myself starting to blush so I change the subject. "Who's Marlow?"

The amusement in Vin's eyes vanishes. "Marlow is the King of The Hive."

"He's basically Vin's boss's boss's boss."

"Wait," I say, looking to Vin. "You're that high up in The Hive?"

"You're surprised?"

"I thought you were a Stable Boy."

"I told you, I'm *The* Stable Boy."

"I don't know what the difference is? Is there

one?"

"It means he's a big deal," Nats explains. "He's kind of like the gang's banker. So going back without Breanne is going to be like losing money. It doesn't look good."

"What will happen to you?" I ask him quietly.

He smirks. "You worried about me?"

"Maybe a little. What will happen?"

"Nothing," he says coolly, looking at Nats. "Cause we're gonna tell them she's dead."

Nats nods solemnly in agreement.

"That seems extreme," I tell him. "Can't you tell him she doesn't want to come back?"

"No. She belongs to the gang. Time, effort and resources have gone into her."

"What? Like food and water? She owes her life for that?"

"Food, water, shelter, soap, clothing and medicine. The women in the stables are the healthiest people in The Hive and these days that doesn't come cheap."

"If you're so high ranking how are you okay with losing her?"

"Because I'm the one who would have to deal with her if we took her back. It's fine for the King to want to keep all of his women at any cost, but the reality falls on me. I'd have to work with a woman who's been to the other side and loved it. Can you imagine what a nightmare it would be to get her working again after she's lived like this?"

I look at Nats. "But you're okay with it? You'll go back?"

She grins. "I don't like cages any more than you do. But Breanne is good with them. Especially gilded ones."

"But aren't you owned by The Hive? Isn't that a cage?"

"Nats has paid her debts in full and she keeps it that way," Vin tells me. "She can walk at any time. She's free."

"And you choose to stay?"

"Where else would I go?" she asks softly, yawning. "Alright, kids, I'm going to work. Find a way to get us out of here, would you?"

"You got it, Nats."

"Later," I call, watching her walk away.

"You're already healthy," Vin says, watching me with a sly smile. "You'd be out of debt and free in no time."

I groan. "Give it a rest. What are we gonna do about getting out of here? You got a plan yet?"

"You need to keep sewing or join the laundry crew," he says, turning serious. "We need more clothes than they'll ever give us at one time. It doesn't have to be sweaters and jackets, but we need layers at least."

I glance at the balled up material of my almost child's shirt and shake my head. "I think I'd better switch to laundry."

"I think you should stay where you are."

"Why?"

"Because of the girl."

"I don't know what her deal is, though. I seem to know more than she does and that's assuming she's not a spy. What if she's working for Caroline and her crew? What if everything she says and does is a test?"

"Then you better not fail."

I glower at him. "That's not helpful at all. What does that even mean?"

"Look, you're smart, Kitten," he says, scratching

his head lazily. "You'll figure it out. I have faith in you."

"Alright, fine, I'll make friends with her."

"Good. You need to start playing in all their reindeer games or you're going to end up an outcast. That looks more suspicious than anything."

I scowl at him. "Are you quoting Christmas songs at me?"

"It's that time of year," he says with a smile.

"Ugh, don't remind me."

He chuckles. "Not a fan of Christmas?"

"No. I hate it."

"What if I promise to get you something pretty this year? Something shiny? Will that get you in the holiday spirit?"

"Just don't get me a Cabbage Patch doll and we're all good."

"Deal."

Chapter Fourteen

The next day I take one for the team; I tell Melissa I've found my calling in the sewing room. She's genuinely excited, smiling at me like I just told her I found Jesus when what I've actually committed to is learning to make socks. Have you ever made a sock? From scratch? Don't, it sucks. But it guarantees me time with my future best friend, Lexy, so I do it.

"You have to pull the thread through tightly but not so tightly that it snaps or bunches the material," Lexy drones.

"We think a Pod was overrun with Risen because the population exploded over night," I tell her quietly, touching the sock as though I'm examining it. As though I give a crap about it. "One day there was barely a zombie in sight, the next it was like the old days. A fallen Pod is the only thing that makes sense."

I listen to the sound of her breathing evenly but I watch as her hands stumble with her work. "It could have been one of your gangs."

"Not possible. There's only one gang in the area big enough and it's still intact. Also, there were children."

"You don't have children on the outside?"

"Some of the gangs do, the ones who keep women, but not this many. Why aren't there children here?"

"This Pod was abandoned for a while. We just reclaimed it. They selected groups of us from other Pods to come and build this new one up again. It was a lot of hard work with long hours and tough labor. And there are so many Risen here. It's too dangerous for children."

"Why was it abandoned?"

"They said there was a plumbing problem."

I stare at her in amazement. "A plumbing problem."

"Yeah."

"And you believed that?"

Lexy looks at me, her face offended. "Why wouldn't I?"

"Because it's dumb. It's the dumbest thing I've ever heard."

"Thanks a lot," she grumbles, playing with her sock.

"Look, just think about that. They cleared out this entire place over a plumbing issue? Who even has plumbing to have an issue with anymore? It's ridiculous."

"If this entire place was flooding with sewage, you would stay?" she asks sharply. "With children and everything. You would tell everyone to stick it out?"

"Not the children, no, but someone would have stayed with the animals and the farming and greenhouse. All of that is way too precious to bail on over a little bit of crap."

"I don't think it was just a little bit."

"Whatever, it's too much to lose," I insist. "The

whole place couldn't have been abandoned over that."

"Maybe it wasn't. Maybe some people stuck around to keep it functioning while it was cleaned up. I don't know. It doesn't matter. Can we make this sock now?"

I look at the directions and shake my head. "You probably can, but I can't. Wait, so if you're all from different Pods, how do you not know how many there are? Can't you get together and say 'Hi, my name is Lexy and I've been held prisoner in Safeco.' Then somebody else does the same and eventually you find out how many there are. Easy."

She looks up at me, her eyes annoyed. Still, she hands me a roll of thread and glances behind me at the other women in the room.

"Some of us have talked," she whispers. "We've tried to get an idea of how many there are but it's tough. They name the Pods with numbers and letters, nothing sequential."

"What's this one?"

"Pod A-63. I came from Pod C-92 which is the football stadium, some others are from G-11, Safeco, and G-35 is farther south on the eastern shore. So far we've counted groups from 4 different Pods but the names are all over the place. They can't be sequential because even if each letter stopped at 100 Pods, that would mean there are at least 700 of them out there each with over 200 people inside almost every one."

I frown. "There aren't 200 people here."

"186," Lexy says without hesitation. "I've counted. Think of the rotations. We're never all in the same place at the same time so of course it doesn't feel like that many."

"If there were that many Pods with 200 people

each, you'd be looking at a population of 140,000 people in this area. That's impossible."

She shakes her head firmly. "I don't think there are that many. I think they label them like that to throw us off. If they called them Pods 1, 2, 3, 4, 5, then we'd all know how many there were or at least have an idea. This way, we have no clue. Maybe there are only 4. Maybe there are 15. We can't know."

"Shady. But what does any of this have to do with me? You wanted information from the outside world but what exactly are you looking for?"

Her eyes dart around the room and I imagine she's taking in every face before speaking. She's quick, I'll give her that. It keeps me wondering if I should even be talking to her.

"You know about the gangs, right?"

"Some things, yeah. Not their secret handshakes or anything, but I've picked up some stuff."

"Is it true about The Hive? Is it the largest gang?"

"By far, yeah."

"Can the hornet be trusted?" she whispers.

"Vin?" I chuckle. "No."

She frowns. "He's your friend, though, right? You trust him."

"Yes and no. It depends what you're trusting him with."

She squares her shoulders and sits back from me. "That's between him and I."

I laugh. I don't mean to laugh in her face, but it's funny to me somehow. This mild mannered girl trying to teach me how to sew is playing tough guy and demanding a private audience with my buddy the pimp. Vin will eat her alive and spit her back out.

"Why are you laughing?" she asks indignantly.

173

I put my hand over my eyes briefly, shaking my head. "I don't know. It's not particularly funny. It's also not going to happen."

"Why not?"

I lower my hand and look her in the eyes. "I'll ask you again; what do you want to talk to Vin about?"

She doesn't answer.

"That right there is why," I tell her. "I'm not going to take you to him. What if you say something ridiculous and he never lets me hear the end of it? I can't live with that, Lexy."

"It's not ridiculous," she says hotly. "It's actually very important."

I shake my head. "I have zero faith in humanity. You need to prove it or go to him yourself. Or are you scared to do that?"

When she looks away I know that's what it is. All of the rumors they tell these people about the gangs has her terrified to speak to him alone. She won't go near him without me and that's a huge problem for her because I don't trust her enough to take her anywhere near him with 'very important' topics.

***

"You cock blocking me, Kitten?"

I sigh. "Given the chance, yes I would. But I don't think she wants that kind of conversation with you."

"One never knows what lies in the interiors of a woman's heart," he muses, swirling his hand elegantly through the air, looking at me with half-lidded eyes. "What desires reside within."

I look at Nats. She's smiling and shaking her head over her eggs.

"What is this?" I ask her. "What is he doing?"

"Pressing your buttons," she chuckles. "Give her a break, Vin."

"Fine," he groans, sitting forward. "What do you think she wants?"

"I don't know yet, but whatever it is, she wants it from you and only you."

"Gotta be something to do with The Hive. We're all from the outside, but if she's looking for me specifically, it's the only thing that sets me apart."

"Is there anything she could want that they'd actually be willing to give her?"

"Not likely," he laughs. "And it doesn't matter. Once I'm outta here, I'm never coming back so whatever she wants, I'm not the guy to deliver."

"*We're* never coming back," Nats corrects, glaring at him.

"Right, yeah. Sorry. Once *we're* out, *we're* never coming back."

I look to Nats. "Is he going to…"

"Double cross us? Probably."

I shake my head at him. "Nice."

"Nothing's been decided yet," he says dismissively.

"That's your defense?"

Nats shrugs. "At least he's honest."

"Don't give him points for that." I jab my finger in his grinning face. "No points!"

"Is there a problem here?"

Caroline. That woman's voice could give me a cavity. She's standing directly behind me, and tell me that's not intentional on her part. She knows about my issues with personal space and right now she's crowding it hard, her hands taking hold of the back of my chair and brushing my back. I suppress a shiver.

"We're fine, Caroline," Vin says, looking at her hard.

"Are you sure?" She leans her weight on her hands on the back of my chair. I can feel her body closing in on mine. I have to grit my teeth to keep from screaming. "It was getting awful loud over here."

"It was a lively discussion." Vin stands and comes around the table to face her. He pushes into her space, forcing her off my back. "It's nothing to worry about."

Caroline laughs falsely. "I never worry about you."

"Good. I think your girls are looking for you."

"Hmm. Will you be looking for me later?"

"Ugh," I groan.

Vin puts his hand on my shoulder and squeezes hard. I shut my trap.

"No," he says firmly.

The silence coming from behind me is deafening. I look to Nats but she's carefully pretending she doesn't hear or see any of this. I try to do the same. It's hard though with Vin's Kung Fu grip on my shoulder.

"Are you sure about that?"

Vin doesn't answer.

"Interesting choice," Caroline whispers.

I feel fingers thread through my hair, pulling it gently. Vin's hand tightens on my shoulder. It would probably hurt if I weren't a statue made of solid stone, frozen in place. Seconds pass and I feel it when Caroline leaves, even before Vin loosens his hold on me. I take a deep breath. Some of the tension leaves me but there's so much, too much, and I don't know how long it will be until I come down entirely.

"Vin," Nats says softly.

"I know." He puts his free hand on my other shoulder so he's holding both of them. He rubs them gently like a massage but I don't even think he knows he's doing it. "I made a mistake."

"Sleeping with Satan?" I mumble.

"For starters," Nats answers. "You should probably take your hands off her. You'll only make it worse."

Vin jerks his hands off my shoulders as though I'd burned him. "You're right. Hell. Sorry, Kitten."

"It's alright." I turn around to look up at him. His face is dark, troubled. "What mistake did you make?"

"I touched you to shut you up but she took it wrong."

"She thinks you're the reason she won't be seeing him tonight. You're back on her radar."

"Oh come on," I moan.

"I said I was sorry. I wasn't thinking."

"Fat lot of good that will do me when there's a knife in my neck."

His troubled expression shifts to angry. "If you'd kept your mouth shut it wouldn't have happened."

"That chick makes me ill, okay? I couldn't keep quiet. You're lucky I didn't lose my dinner all over the table. And don't blame me. If you'd keep it in your pants this wouldn't be a problem in the first place."

"She's right, Vin."

"Shut up, both of you," he barks. "I apologized twice already, what do you want?"

"No," I correct him. "You said you were sorry and you referenced the sorry, but you did not apologize twice. I'll take extra groveling. Let's have it."

"Not gonna happen," he says dryly, walking away. "You only get one."

"No points!"

Chapter Fifteen

A week goes by and I have no problems with Caroline. That actually bothers me. She's sitting back, waiting for something, but for what I'm not sure. If she's waiting for me to drop my guard, she's testing the wrong girl. I've lived the majority of my life on the outside where everyone and everything is trying to kill me all day every day. My guard doesn't know how to drop.

Lexy starts avoiding me so I work with some of the other women in the sewing room. They're alright, but Lexy bothers me. I guess whatever she wanted wasn't so important or she'd be pushing the issue. I'm left feeling kind of disappointed and very annoyed. I'm locked in here now because of her and she doesn't even want to play ball anymore.

"Joss."

I hear my name whispered as I'm leaving the cafeteria to start my work shift. When I glance around, I find Amber in a dark doorway to the kitchen waving me to her.

"Hey, what's up?" I say, walking over.

"Shh," she whispers, glancing around. "Come on, hurry. Before someone sees."

I follow obediently into the kitchen to find the whole crew there tucked in the back corner around a small table. The previous work crew is still buzzing around like their shift isn't ending.

"Joss," Steven beams, though I do note he does it quietly. There's a hushed air in the kitchen that sets me on edge. Even the girl washing dishes is doing it softly.

"Hi," I reply, my tone guarded.

"We've missed you in here."

"Really?"

He smiles. "Yes, of course. And we have a surprise for you."

I stop a few steps from them. "I don't really do well with surprises."

Everyone chuckles quietly.

"Understood," Steven replies.

Amber approaches me slowly with a plate clearly presented before her. "He made a pie."

And there it is. Pumpkin, shiny, creamy, beautiful. I almost bury my face in the plate in her hands like a rabid dog seeing its first meal in days, but I'm able to hold it together. I drool a little, that's all. That's respectable, right?

"Seriously? A real pie?"

"With contraband sugar and everything."

"Don't tell anyone though," Steven reminds me as I take the plate reverently from Amber's outstretched hands. "It's a forbidden pie."

"Even better." I dip the fork into the smooth, orange wonder and bring it slowly to my mouth. It dissolves on my tongue almost immediately and my legs go weak. "Oh God."

"Right?" Crystal says with a smile. "You should sit down."

I smile in return, taking an offered seat. "I think I have to. Steven, this is amazing."

"Thank you."

"What's the occasion?" I ask, devouring another bite. The Colonies have never been so tempting.

Steven exchanges a look with Amber and Crystal. I instantly go back on alert. But I don't stop eating the pie. Priorities.

"We have an important question to ask you," he says.

I chuckle. "Everything here is so important. What's up? What do you need from me?"

"Why won't the hornet talk to Lexy?"

I freeze, my fork nearly in my mouth. I carefully glance around the room, checking to see who is listening.

"It's alright," Steven says confidently. "They're fine."

I put my fork down. "Fine in what way exactly?"

"In the sense that you don't have to censor yourself here."

"I don't know what you're talking about."

"You don't have to play coy with us." He pats my hand reassuringly. It makes me squirm. "We all know everything about it."

I pull my hand away. "Then you know more than I do. What exactly are we talking about here?"

Steven looks unsure for a moment. "Lexy approached you, correct?"

"She attacked me in my sleep one night, yeah."

"We heard about that," Amber says. "That was a bad choice."

"That's what I thought."

"But she has explained to you why she did it,

yes?' Steven presses.

I shake my head. "No. I mean, I know she wants to talk to Vin but she won't say what it's about. Doesn't really make me want to take her to him, you know?"

Steven sighs as he removes his hat to rub his bald head. He mutters, "She's excessive with the cloak and dagger routine."

"She doesn't know her like we do," Crystal insists.

"Then they should have had us do this in the first place."

"You know why they couldn't. Why we shouldn't be doing this now."

"I thought everyone in here was cool," I interrupt, getting annoyed.

"They are," Steven replies defensively.

"Then what's with all the vaguery."

Amber frowns. "That's not a word."

"Do you understand what I mean by it?"

"Yes."

"Then it's a word, isn't it? Answer the question. What do you guys want from Vin? And who am I talking about when I say 'you guys'?"

Steven shifts uncomfortably in his seat. "We weren't supposed to talk to you about this."

"Vaguery!"

"Shh, alright," Crystal says, sounding annoyed. "There's a group of us, a rather large group, who are not especially happy with our current situation."

"Your situation with the Colonies?"

"Our situation at *this* Colony," Steven corrects.

"How is this one different than any others?"

"The first Colony was incredible. It was a lifesaver. People joined up willingly and it grew and grew until we had to branch out. New Colonies were formed, new Pods created. We traded with each other, we visited one another. You were allowed to go outside the gates and be in the world. It was dangerous but it was nice to walk free, to swim in the Sound, to visit the city. But as the Colonies expanded more and more, the tone of things changed. They stopped talking about surviving and being a community. It became more about keeping the sickness out and maintaining the purity within. The doors were locked, people were assigned permanently to Pods and we lost contact with everyone else. Then the roundups started. They went into the city and gathered people, saying we were saving them from themselves and the illness. They were put to work. If they refused, they were taken away. People would disappear for days, sometimes weeks, and they'd come out looking broken. But they'd get right to work. It's been going on this way for years."

"That's a generalization of all Colonies," I say, feeling annoyed. "You said you're unhappy with this one specifically. So you're okay with all of that stuff? With being locked in and the roundups and us from the outside being taken prisoner?"

"It's a posh prison compared to outside."

"It's still a prison," I tell him hotly. "Just because you don't want out doesn't mean it's not a cage."

"But you see, we do want out. Or at least to go back home. When they brought all of us here to fix this place up, they broke up families, something they'd never done before. They pulled parents from children, husbands from wives, sisters from brothers. They say the selection system is a lottery, that it's random, but it's not. It's very specific."

"Separating you from your families keeps you in line doesn't it? It gives you the incentive to keep your head down."

He nods grimly. When I glance at the others I can the tension in their faces. They're all missing someone. "It's a very good incentive, yes. One that we believe they felt the need to implement only recently. You see, Lexy told us your theory about the fallen Pod. We think you're right."

"Really? Because she didn't seem to believe me. Or she didn't want to."

"She's skeptical of everything," Crystal says with distaste. "That's why she's dropped the ball with you."

"What does that mean?"

"She was supposed to convince you to let her speak to the hornet a week ago. She's not even trying anymore, is she?"

"No, she's avoiding me actually."

Crystal shakes her head, disgusted.

"Why didn't you guys approach me?" I ask. "I would have taken any one of you to him immediately."

"We were told not to talk to you about it."

"By who? The Team Leaders?"

Steven chuckles. "No. By the others. Others like us."

"Others who are unhappy?" I ask, picking up on what we're not saying.

He nods. "But we got on with you too well too fast. It's why Melissa pulled you out of here. She likes your relationship with Lexy because you don't like each other. You obviously don't trust each other."

"And Melissa knows all of this how?"

"We're watched very closely. This right now is actually very dangerous which is why any further communication will have to be with Lexy."

"How can you go along with this?" I ask exasperated. "If you know they're manipulating you and kidnapping people like me, how can you still be in favor of the Colonies?"

"We're not in favor of it. Not exactly. We're not ready to go out and live in the wild like you do, none of us would last a day, but we do want the old days of the Colonies. Back when it was a community all about survival and not—"

"A prison? A slave trade?"

Steven's mouth drops into a grim line but he nods. "Yes, exactly."

"As long as you're in favor of people like me being allowed to live their life as they choose—"

"We are."

"Then we're good. I'm on board. But you still haven't answered me, though I think I know the answer already. What does Lexy want to talk to Vin about?"

Steven meets my eyes with a sad smile. "Freedom."

I nod. "I think that's a conversation Vin would be willing to have."

***

"Are you for real?" Vin asks Lexy, staring at her in amazement.

"Don't be a dick," I mutter to him.

I would rather he didn't burn this bridge just as I built it up. It took days to get Lexy talking to me. Days of sitting beside her working on seams and never saying anything about my conversation in the kitchen.

They told me to wait, to let her come to me. To let her take her time until she was ready. Steven and the rest of the kitchen crew promised to talk to Lexy and explain my willingness to bring her to Vin now that I knew what was what, at least a little. Still she made me wait.

Finally, on day four of the silent treatment, she broke down and asked again to speak to the hornet. I wanted to tell her no, just to watch her head explode. But I was too frustrated to bother, so I told her I would make it happen.

The wild is very straightforward. All of this intrigue and drama here on the inside is giving me hives.

"No, really, I need to know," Vin demands, having listened to her tell him the story the kitchen crew told me. "Is she being serious? Am I insane or am I getting this right? Because she isn't actually saying what she wants."

"I've made myself very clear," Lexy says angrily.

I put my hand up to stop her. "Don't fight fire with fire where Vin is concerned. You'll only get burned." I turn to face Vin, trying to be patient. "She hasn't been clear, no, but you get the idea."

He ignores me and glares at Lexy. "Say it in plain English or go away."

I watch her grit her teeth but she doesn't walk. I'm a little shocked by that. "We want help from The Hive."

"Help with what?"

"With our release." She takes a breath and her voice softens. "You're not the only prisoners here."

Vin chuckles darkly. "Honey, they won't even help with my release. They don't care anything about yours."

"Why not? Your people hate the Colonies. I'd think they'd jump at the chance to take one down."

Vin snorts. "Not badly enough to risk the lives of everyone in The Hive. If they come here and you don't succeed, they'll all be taken prisoner as well. It's not worth it. Not by a long shot." He leans forward and folds his hands on the table, looking her hard in the eye with his charming smile. "Now, if you want to free me, I'm all for that. I'll go ask them to come rushing back here, but don't be surprised when no one shows."

"Not even you?" Lexy asks, glancing at Nats and I sitting on either side of Vin. "Not even for them?"

"Not for anyone," he replies, no hesitation.

She shakes her head. "I can't believe that."

"Believe it," I tell her. "It's how it is in the wild. It's how you survive."

"Kitten's right. You can't value anyone or anything too much."

"Which is why you have to offer The Hive more. Way more than just Vin or a shot at destroying this place," I say evenly, wondering what the hell I'm doing.

But I've been thinking about this for the last four days as I waited for Lexy to decide she trusted me. I figured it out that they wanted Vin for his connection to The Hive and since they wanted their freedom, what else could they be planning but to ask The Hive to attack this small Pod and set them all free? And I knew it would never work. I didn't have the heart to tell them that because I want to hope too, I want to believe that I'll make it out of here someday even if it's childish to dream of it. That's when I started wondering if there was a way.

"What are you talking about?" Vin asks slowly, eyeing me.

"What could we give them?" Lexy asks warily.

"You'll give them the one thing they'll fight for," I tell her. "You'll give them this Pod. Intact. Undamaged. Taken down from the inside. That's something they could *never* have, not without you."

Vin sits back hard in his chair, watching me. I can see the wheels turning, the numbers crunching and the idea forming in his mind. But will it be enough?

I look at Lexy but I'm speaking to Vin. "There's hardly any leadership here because they have you all over a barrel with your families. From what I understand, there's enough unrest to overthrow this place from the inside. So do it. Take control and ask The Hive to help you take down the next Pod in exchange for ownership over this one. If they attacked it from the outside without your help, they'd damage the hell out of it. It'd be almost worthless to them later."

"There are plans in place to destroy it and escape, leaving attackers nothing to show for their efforts," Lexy confirms.

"Exactly. They'd gain nothing. But if you hand it to them, they could actually use it. They wouldn't just be a gang anymore, they'd be an outpost. It's a whole different level of living than what they've got right now. With the resources you have, it would set them head and shoulders above the rest of the gangs out there. They'd be the Walmart of the wild. Once you take down the next Pod, you'll have their numbers, your families, added to your ranks. You wouldn't necessarily need The Hive anymore to take down the third one. But even if you did, you still have a bargaining chip."

"The second Pod?" Lexy asks, looking very, very interested.

"No. Knowledge. They have no idea how to take care of this place. They don't plant crops or tend fields, not on this level, and they don't have livestock. They fish and go to market to trade for whatever else they need. Ask Vin if he can milk a cow. I promise you he can't and I doubt any of his crew can either. But you can. You said it yourself, you didn't need a lot of leadership cause you're all veterans here. Use that to your advantage to leverage more help from The Hive."

Lexy looks at me hopefully, then turns to Vin. "Would they do it? Would they agree to help us if we gave up a Pod?"

"And promised an end to the roundups," I supply, thinking that's a practice I'd rather The Hive didn't adopt once they gained this seat of power.

"Would that all be worth it to them?"

Vin clears his throat. I watch as he spins his ring on his finger, thinking.

"I don't know for sure. But it would certainly be worth a shot," he replies quietly.

Lexy's brow falls. She looks unsure as she glances at me. "Is that good enough? Can I trust him?"

"Probably not."

"Brutal, Kitten," he mutters.

"But what choice do you have?" I ask Lexy, ignoring Vin and his feelings. "You can't sit around waiting for more gang members to show up here and hope they'll play ball."

"More of them have shown up. Just last week. But they're from smaller gangs and wouldn't be any use."

"Wait, there are more outsiders here? Since

when?" I ask, sitting forward.

I can feel Vin watching me closely, thinking of other things now.

"Since last week," Lexy replies. "They're on the second schedule. It's just two of them from some small gang."

"What do they look like?"

"I don't know. I haven't seen them. I only heard about them."

"Can you find out their names for me?"

"Sure," Lexy nods. "I'll see what I can do if you talk to him about doing this for us."

Vin puts his hands up innocently. "I already said I'd plead your case to The Hive if you freed me."

"Yeah, but it didn't exactly sound like you were planning on selling it," Nats says, glaring at him.

"Are you mad at me right now?" he asks incredulously.

"We all are. It's a good deal and you know they'll consider it. They would kill to get their hands on a piece of the Colonies. You'll be Marlow's Golden Boy if you bring this to him so stop playing coy and just agree to it." Vin goes to open his mouth but before he can speak Nats points her finger at him, whispering fiercely, "And you better come back for me, you son of a bitch. You leave me here to rot in this cage and I'll die of boredom and haunt you for the rest of your days."

Vin grins affectionately at her hostility. He leans forward to kiss her cheek lightly. "Anything you say, Boss."

"So you'll do it?" Lexy asks eagerly. "You'll go for help?"

He nods reluctantly at her. "Yeah, I'll do it. Just

tell me when and my bags will be packed."

"Tomorrow night," she says without hesitation.

"What?" I ask, shocked. "Seriously?"

"Yes, we're ready. We've been ready. There's no sense in waiting, right?"

"I guess not," I mutter, still feeling surprised by the suddenness of it. How long have they had this planned just waiting for the right person to set free?

"You'll go out on a boat. I can't get you a jacket, they monitor those too closely and only hand them out to people working the fields. Then they take them back the second they come inside. But the women in the laundry have been pulling things aside in varying sizes so you can wear layers."

"You've been prepping for this already?" Vin asks. "Even before asking me?"

Lexy shrugs with a smile. "Luck favors the prepared."

The phrase immediately reminds me of Crazy Crenshaw and I realize I miss him and his madness. Among other things.

"How exactly am I getting out?"

"Tim will explain all that in the morning. He's got an idea of how to slip you through the fences."

"Tim from the field crew? He's in on this?"

"We're all in on this," Lexy says seriously. "Every last one of us."

***

As it turns out, that's not strictly true. Aside from the meager leadership, there are still a few people in this Pod that are too scared of the Colony's rule to stand up against it. Hopefully when it all goes down they'll jump on board anyway. At that point, what have they got to lose? But until then some stealth is still required and even Lexy isn't 100% sure who is a total ally and who isn't. Aside from herself, Tim, a few of his friends in the fields, all of the women in the laundry, half the sewing room, all of the kitchen and the better part of the greenhouse and gardens crew, people's alliances are unknown. That means every last guard is a question mark and most likely loyal to the Colony, albeit grudgingly.

Ask me how much I like those odds.

But the ball is rolling and after dinner Lexy took off to tell Tim and the others heading this thing that Vin is on board. I wonder if she's going to tell them how shady it all is, that we don't know for sure if The Hive will bite. That we don't know if Vin will ever come back.

"You look worried, Kitten," Vin tells me from across the table.

Nats has gone to work while Vin and I are skipping out on after dinner family fun time in the common room. There are a few other people here in the cafeteria with us sitting around tables alone or in small groups, chatting quietly.

"Shouldn't I be?" I ask dryly.

"You worried about me? That I'm gonna get hurt?"

"No," I chuckle.

"You worried about your boy?"

I frown at him. "What?"

"Are you worried he's one of the newbies she told you about?"

Yes. I am worried Ryan is here. I'm worried he's here and I'm hoping he's here and the contradiction is ridiculous and torturous.

"No."

"You're a terrible liar."

"You're a terrible person."

He grins. "You don't mean that."

"Are you really going to do it?" I ask him, staring him straight in the eye. "Will you really go to Marlow and try and sell this to him? Or will you go home and forget about us?"

His grin fades. He spins the ring on his finger and I wonder what he's considering. Lying to me? Telling me the cold, hard truth? Or is he actually wondering what he'll do? Part of me wonders if he, as cocky and sure as he is, even knows what will come of this night.

"We'll have to wait and see, won't we?" he finally replies, his voice deep and low.

I should be annoyed with him. Even to me, the loner of loners, it's a no brainer. If the Colonies can be stopped, we have to try. It'll mean one less worry in the wild. One less predator to be afraid of every second of every day. It could even mean the trading of Colony goods, something that would benefit every last one of us outside these walls. But I'm not annoyed because I understand. I get the mentality of every man for himself and this help your fellow man for the greater good business is a notion that died out a decade ago. It was spilled with blood and lost to the ground in the first bite of the first zombie to rise up from the dead and usher in the dawn of the Hell on Earth that we walk in today.

Welcome to the apocalypse.

This is the world we live in now and it's been working relatively well for everyone so far. We're all still alive, aren't we?

Honestly, are we?

I don't know anymore. I think of the last message I wrote to Ryan telling him I was waking up. I still believe it, even here and now in this place where everyone seems to be sheep falling asleep, following commands. No part of me wants to fall in line, not even with Vin when it's for the greater good. I don't know if that makes me a loner, a rebel or a free thinker who refuses to go down without a fight. Maybe I'm none of them or maybe I'm all of them, but what I know for certain is that I need to leave this place to find out. I want another shot at living my life outside with choices to be made and risks to be taken. I want to laugh out loud with no one else around. I want to walk through the streets and not be so afraid of who sees me. And I want to write on the wall with no filter or restraint.

"I have to go," I say suddenly, heading for the door.

"Not even going to kiss me goodbye?!" Vin calls after me.

I run through the halls and burst outside, the cold air slapping me hard in the face. It invades my lungs, pinching them and making it painful to breathe. I don't envy Vin this. Going out into this cold tomorrow. Trying to make it across the city is going to suck for him. Lexy told us it's about a mile and a half from here to aquarium but it's going to be dark, possibly raining and so very cold. We didn't even discuss the massive swarm of Risen roaming just outside the walls. Luckily Vin thinks he's invincible.

"You're not supposed to be out here," I hear a voice say to me from across the grass.

I raise my hand, waving to them faintly. "Sorry, I

just... I needed some air. I won't leave this spot okay? Just five minutes?"

The guard hesitates and I wish I knew some of them. I wish I'd made more friends and had more pull. Don't tell Vin.

Finally he nods silently and goes on about his patrol, but I know he won't go very far. That's okay. This won't take long.

I look around the ground furtively, cursing the sparseness of this area, but this is as far out as I can get. Whatever I find in here is going to have to suit me. What I could do is go inside and forget the whole thing. It's not like it matters. It's not like he'll ever see it. It's not like he's here.

My heart pangs at the idea of him locked inside these walls and I want to write this message more than ever if only to prove to myself that it will go unnoticed. That he's not here. Finally I spot a small stone that looks like it will do. I snatch it up in my trembling, cold fingers. Then I write. I write with simple honesty something I would never have had the nerve to write on the outside but wish desperately that I had. It's nothing huge. Nothing profound. But it's heartfelt and real and I imagine as I write it on this wall in this prison that the words are appearing on our wall on the outside. That this message will reach him no matter where he is. That he'll think of me and that sliver of my soul that I left with him to travel wherever he goes will light up like the sun and run with him again. He'll carry me far away from here, outside these walls, beyond these waters and I'll be home again. Just four words to fly me away forever.

I miss your kiss.

Chapter Sixteen

That night I don't think any of us sleep. I see Lexy before going to bed and when I ask her if she's gotten the names of the new gang members in the Pod, she shakes her head sadly. Tim has never seen them either, only heard of them. She tells me they're from a gang called The Elevens, some reference to the Eleventh Hour, but I've never heard of it. I never got the name of Ryan's gang anyway. I'm more convinced with each passing second that he is one of them and the writing I left on the wall is burning in my mind like a brand. I'm dying to walk past it but terrified as well. What if there's a response?

I decide to lie down and toss and turn in my bed instead.

At least that's the plan, until a hand clasps over my mouth. Second time since I've been here and I still don't like it. When my eyes pop open I come face to face with Vin, his handsome features shrouded in darkness giving him a sinister quality.

But I know it's him. I'm know I'm safe.

So why do I backhand him across the face? Because he knows better, that's why.

He doesn't cry out as Lexy did when I hit him or even as Ryan did when I punched him for messing up my night. He simply looks away for a moment, takes a calming breath and looks back at me with hard eyes.

"You think I deserved that?" he asks tightly.

"If not for startling me awake then I'm sure somewhere at some point in your life you earned that," I whisper angrily.

"Fair enough. Come on."

"Where?"

"Outside." He stands, offering me his hand. "We have to talk."

I ignore his hand but I follow him out of the dark room, leaving the soft sounds of even breathing and light snoring behind us. He leads me silently through the hallways and out the door, the same door I burst out of earlier tonight. It's even colder now. I can see my breath coming in small puffs of white in front of me. There's no one patrolling nearby and I imagine we have a small window of opportunity to talk and freeze before the next guard comes by.

"Merry Christmas," he says quietly, pulling something from his back pocket.

I frown in confusion, then smile in delight when I see what it is. It's a shiny, sharp trowel with a holly green handle. It's stolen from the gardens for sure. It is the single greatest gift I've ever received.

"It's so pretty," I whisper happily, turning it over to test its edge.

"I promised you something shiny."

"And you delivered." I press my finger against the tip then pull it back quickly. "It's sharp."

"Why else have it, right? Keep it with you when you can. If something goes down while I'm gone, I want to know you have it."

I nod my head as I slip it into my back pocket. The

handle sticks up but the point is hidden.

When I look up at Vin my heart skips. His eyes are sharp, intense.

"Come with me," he commands quietly.

"No," I reply immediately.

I was waiting for this. From the moment he woke me up, the second I saw his eyes, I knew. And just as quickly as I recognized it, I knew what my answer would be.

He shakes his head in disbelief. "You know I'm not coming back here. Not for you, not for anyone."

"Maybe not, but if I go with you then you definitely won't."

"It's not going to work, Joss," he tells me seriously. "The Hive won't bite. They don't want to rock the boat with the Colonies and the pot isn't sweet enough to convince them to try. They'll pass and everyone here is going to either stay here forever or die in a revolt."

"Nats included," I remind him coolly.

"She's a big girl. She knows how it really is. She can yell at me all she wants, but she knows just as well as I do that no one will come here to help."

"Especially if you don't ask."

"What the hell do you want from me?" he whispers fiercely. "You want me to go out there and rally the troops, bring them back here riding on a tall white horse and save the day? I'm no hero. I never have been. It's how I've stayed alive."

"It's also a great way to stay alone. And if you do this, if you go and pretend we don't exist, then I'll pretend I never knew you. Nats will too, I'm sure. You'll be nothing to no one and won't that make life easier for you? So go on and go, you coward, and don't ever look back because there's nothing to look back on. You were never even here far as I'm concerned."

I turn to leave him standing there in the cold beside the words I wrote to Ryan, words that have gone unnoticed and feel like nothing in the night. I'm spun around roughly and pinned against Vin's chest. His breath is coming even and hard, sharp inhales and exhales that burst against my face leaving my skin freezing in their absence.

"Don't turn your back on me," he growls.

I can see the enforcer in him now. The killer who lived on the outside by the skin of his teeth and grit under his knuckles. It's something I understand, something I can respect. Something I can relate to.

I lean closer, no longer being pulled but rather pushing against him until our faces almost touch.

"No, don't *you* turn your back on *me*. On *us*," I whisper harshly, pushing at him aggressively. He lets me go and I stumble back from him.

"I'm no hero," he repeats.

"How do you know until you've tried?"

"You expect too much of me," he says quietly. It could be a trick of the light, but I swear his eyes look sad.

"I expect you to be a man," I say harshly. "Not a great one, not even a good one. Just a man. A little bit of bravery and a little bit of honor. That's all I'm asking."

He shakes his head at me, running his hands over his hair. It's growing out again. It's getting longer and he's looking less like the Vin I've gotten to know in here and more like the guy from the outside.

"I don't know what I'm gonna do when I get out, Kitten," he tells me softly. He's not looking at me and it somehow makes me trust him more. "I have no idea. I know what I should do."

"You should walk away," I say, knowing it's true.

"Yeah. I should forget all about all of you. But I don't know if that's what I want to do. I don't know if it's something I can do."

"You're not going to know until you try. That's all any of us can ask of you anyway. We just need you to try."

He looks at me then and it's strange. He doesn't look so much older than me anymore. He looks young and vulnerable, completely unsure.

"What do you think I'll do?" he whispers. "Do you think I'll do the right thing?"

"No," I answer without hesitation.

I'm relieved when he laughs. "Thanks for that."

"I have my doubts, just like you. But the fact that you're torn gives me hope."

"Ooh," he says with a wince. "That is a dirty word, Kitten. You know that."

I step closer to him and wrap my arms around him tightly, shocking him. He hesitates before hugging me back gently. I'm proud of him that his hands stay out of my danger zones.

"You'll come back for us, Vin," I whisper in his ear. "I know you will."

I know no such thing, but I want it to be true and I can tell he does too, so I tell him that it is. I lie to us both and I hope it makes it real.

Vin nods his head beside mine and buries his face in my shoulder. I do the same. We stand huddled together against the cold and the uncertainty of everything tomorrow will bring.

That's why we never see it coming.

Vin is slammed harder against me, pressing me painfully into the wall. When I open my eyes I feel his breath rush out of him in one huge exhale. He groans as his head sags forward, his hands clenching hard against my skin. I'll have bruises later. But that's the least of our worries. I'm looking over his shoulder staring face to face with Caroline. Her eyes are wild and huge, staring straight at me as she leans against Vin's back.

"Should have stayed away from him, whore," she breathes at me.

I watch in shock as she steps back, leaving Vin sagging against me and pulling a long, bloody knife away with her. She's stabbed him. I don't know where and I don't know if it's fatal, but the knowledge shifts my gears. The shock wears off and the autopilot kicks on. When I look at her, I know she knows.

She's made a terrible mistake.

I shove Vin to the side, letting him fall carelessly onto the frozen ground. Then I lunge at her. I don't make contact, I only lunge. I'm testing her reflexes, seeing how she wields the knife. I need answers to a few questions right now and they're all put to rest with that one movement. Her reaction tells me everything I need to know and the simple truth is this: Barbie doesn't have what it takes.

When I lunge at her she jumps back quickly and slashes the knife in front of her. It's a good move, it keeps me away from her. But a better move, one that a person accustomed to working with a weapon and letting it work for them would do, is to meet my lunge with her own and stab at me in close proximity. I can't just take that knife from her, not if I want to keep my blood in my body, and if she's quick and efficient enough she could kill me before I lay a hand on her.

Kind of like this. Watch.

I pull the trowel from my back pocket, holding it at waist level in my right hand. My strong hand. I miss my ASP and its long reach, but autopilot doesn't care. All autopilot wants is to put down the threat and go to bed. So that's what it does. It lunges forward again, backing Caroline up until she stumbles off the walkway and lands on the ground on her back. It watches as she slashes out wildly, hoping to force me back away from her. It waits patiently. Then it lunges again. It stomps on her arm holding the knife, pinning it down. Forcing it to be still. It moves forward, bringing the sharpened trowel down. It sinks it uncontested into Caroline's throat. It watches her eyes go wide, then roll back in her head.

It slips out of the driver's seat.

I shake as I watch her bleed into the ground.

Dead.

Dead at my hand.

Chapter Seventeen

As I feel the adrenaline leave me, I feel the cold sink in deeper. It sets root in my heart and freezes my blood until I can't move, until my muscles atrophy. I'm paralyzed and eggshell fragile. I'm a statue. A porcelain figurine. A killer.

"Kitten."

Vin's weak voice calls to me from far off. I try to ignore it but he won't shut up.

"Kitten."

My eyes gain focus. I find myself staring at Caroline's lifeless corpse. I've seen plenty of dead bodies in my day. A lot of them are actually ones I laid to their final rest. But they were all dead already, all on their way and lost in the confusing haze of being a Risen. I helped them find clarity. Finality.

This is different. This was a living, breathing, seething person until along came a spider who stabbed her in the neck and let her bleed out at her feet. This is ugly and hateful.

Is this me?

"Kitten!"

"What?!" I cry, turning to face him.

I'm actually surprised to find him still alive. I

figured that despite the fact that Caroline was literally a backstabber, she was probably a finish the job kind of girl too. But there he lies, a pool of dark blood seeping out of his side. He's breathing and cursing like any other day of the week.

"You okay?" I ask numbly.

He glares up at me. "Do I fucking look okay?!"

I fall to my knees beside him. "You've looked better."

"What about you?" he wheezes, grasping his side and eyeing me. "Are you okay?"

"I fucking look okay?" I deadpan.

"Was it your first time?"

"Yeah."

"It gets easier."

I snort. "I doubt that."

"Trust me, it does."

"I don't want it to," I say weakly, my eyes stinging.

"It's not really a choice."

I move to glance over my shoulder. To look at Caroline. At my kill.

"Don't," Vin says firmly, gripping my hand with his blood smeared palm.

"What the hell happened?!" a voice cries from the doorway.

Vin and I both look over slowly to find Tim standing there in shock, looking from us to Caroline and back again.

"What?" is all he can muster.

"We ran into a little trouble with the plan," Vin tells him with a grunt.

He keeps moving around. I assume he's trying to ease the pain but it's not going to happen. Not until he's sewn together again. I grab his shirt at the front then yank hard. It rips down the center, tearing in two. I help him pull his arms out of it then ball it up and press it firmly against his wound.

"Vin needs a doctor," I tell Tim. He's staring at Caroline. "She doesn't need anything. Not anymore."

Tim looks at me for a long moment. His face is a mask and I wonder what he's thinking. Can he see it on me that I did it? That I killed her? I feel like it's marked on me somehow, like a stink I'll never be able to wash away.

"Here's what happened," he says quickly and quietly, moving to Caroline's body. "Joss came out here for some fresh air. She saw Vin and Caroline… being intimate. She felt angry and jealous so she attacked Caroline with… what is this in her neck?"

"A trowel," Vin and I say in unison monotone.

"Alright, Joss attacked her with a trowel. She killed Caroline and found the knife that she always kept on her for protection. Then she turned the knife on Vin, stabbed him, took Caroline's keys to the fence and ran."

"I'm leaving?" I ask, looking at him in surprise.

"Hell yes, you're leaving." He's rooting around in Caroline's pockets now, jostling her body back and forth. It flops lifelessly and I worry I'll be sick. "Vin can't go and you can't stay here. You killed one of the leaders. And this is better than Vin escaping. That brings up questions of how and who helped and is there dissension in the ranks. This way it was a lover's quarrel, something not uncommon in the Pods, though it usually ends in fist fights not…"

"Stabbings?" I ask.

"Exactly. Here." Keys land beside my knees on

the packed, frosty dirt. "Take those. Get out of here. Do what he was supposed to do."

I shake my head, staring at the keys. At freedom. "The Hive doesn't know me," I protest weakly. "They'll never listen to me. They'll never even speak to me."

"Take this." Vin pulls his ring off his finger and slips it on mine. On the ring finger of my left hand. He smirks through a grimace. "Don't get excited, it's just a loner."

"Nothing would thrill me less," I mutter, staring at the ring. It's a dark metal full of dents, scratches and dark blue flecks. It's beautiful.

"Yeah," he grunts. "Act like I don't know."

"Will they recognize it?"

"Marlow will. He knows it was my old man's. It's the only thing that's ever meant anything to me."

I look in his eyes and feel like crying. He could die. I could die. We all might die no matter what I do, but suddenly I feel so cold and bone tired I don't even know which way is up anymore.

"They won't listen to me, will they?" I whisper.

His lips form a grim line. He shakes his head sharply. "Probably not."

I nod, looking at the ring and thinking it doesn't matter. None of it matters. Not if we never try.

"Alright, I'll go," I say, standing and quaking with cold and nerves.

"Hey," Vin says. He's staring up at me and in this light I can't read his eyes. "You'll get it done. You're a better man than I am."

I chuckle. "No shit."

Two minutes later I'm wearing Tim's sweater, carrying the knife and trowel and I'm running through the gates. I fumble in the dark, slipping on the wet boards of the dock. Finally I get my hands on a small rowboat and cast off, launching myself out over the cold, black water. If a guard sees me, they don't say anything and I wonder if some of them aren't sick of the Colony after all. It's a miracle I've made it out unseen and unhurt. It'll be an even bigger miracle if I survive.

It's icy cold out here and even with Tim's sweater I'm still shivering violently. It's not just the cold. It's the lack of adrenaline after the fight, it's the shock of having killed a woman, it's the fear for Vin's life, it's the fear for my life and the fear of the Risen that surround this place in a thick wave that comes crashing in on me the second I take to shore.

I have to start running immediately and I can only hope I'm going the right way. Tim told me to head southeast. He said there are roads that are intentionally filled with debris and made impassible to force attacks from only one direction. Southeast.

I run as fast as I can, leaving a pocket of Risen behind and finding a blessed silent section of the city. I know the Risen are surrounding me on all sides, I can hear them everywhere, but I have to get it together. I slow my pace, slow my breathing and try to slow my mind. It's racing ahead of me, running away from me. It's already at The Hive. It's already standing before Marlow, assuming I ever even make it that far without being killed or pimped, and it's failing. It's showing him the ring, he's laughing in its face and he's sending it to the stables. All my worst fears are running around me, after me, before me. I feel so boxed in and terrified that I stop moving entirely to lean over and vomit on the street.

A Risen stumbles in front of me from out of nowhere, though in this darkness everywhere is nowhere. It takes me a moment to get my bearings and it's a moment I don't have. I take an extra second too long to verify that it's dead, that it's not another Caroline, and in that second it grabs me hard. I drop the knife to push on its forehead and keep its gnashing, drooling teeth from closing in on my face. I can smell the putrid breath of the thing rolling over me and I gag hard. I can't get in a clean breath. I'm starting to see stars. I'm wondering what the hell is wrong with me when I finally get it together enough to jam the trowel into the Risen's eye. It's too large to go in far enough to damage the brain so I have to pull it out and try another angle. It will scar me further for the rest of my days, but I do what I know works. I start stabbing the trowel into the neck of the thing, front and back and sides, pushing harder and harder back until it finally does its job. The head falls forward useless as all of the muscles I've cut lose tension and give out. It's drooling over its own chest, unable to look anywhere but at its feet, and as I back away it starts walking in circles looking for me.

I can hear the moan and groan of other Risen falling in close on me from all sides. They smell the blood on me. Caroline's blood. It's all over the shirt beneath Tim's sweater. Even now with that sweater covered in the cold black tar that this zombie just sprayed all over me, they smell Caroline. There are too many here and I don't have the kind of weaponry I need to survive this. Even with my ASP and a gun I don't know if I'd survive this swarm. This is part of the Colony's defenses, I realize. This is just another way they keep us locked in. Or dead.

I give up running. I'm lost in the dark at this point and exhausted beyond reason. I decide to head for the nearest building. It's my only shot, though it's not much of one. I'm shivering and shaking as I sprint clumsily inside, feeling the agonizing press of the walls around me and the hands at my back. They're everywhere, literally everywhere here and I wonder if this wasn't the dumbest idea I've ever had. I make it to the stairwell and start to climb, my legs shaking beneath me. I stumble twice, and each time it's harder to get back up. I can't see a thing in here and I'm working entirely on feel. Do you understand how horrifying that is? Being in the dark, nearly unarmed and surrounded by your worst nightmare. I expect every step to stumble me, every breath to be my last. Every corner holds the promise of stepping straight into the crushing embrace of a hungry risen, primed and ready to devour me with yellow, rotted teeth. They'll sink into my flesh. They'll tear it from the bones. All while I live and breathe and scream.

By the time I burst through the opening to the roof, I'm crying. I'm weeping, nearly hyperventilating and shaking from head to toe. I slam the door behind me, nearly screaming in relief when I find a working lock on it. I don't hear the infected coming, but that doesn't mean they're not. They're down there in the streets below, shuffling and moaning. They were in the building as I ran through. They know where to find me. It's only a matter of time.

I collapse against the door, sinking down onto the rough rooftop. I'm feeling like this is as good a place as any to die. I work harder than I ever have before to find my numb. To get it back, to be the unfeeling, uncrying, unafraid, unaffected husk I have been for the last six years. To be the girl who survives. But I'm not her anymore. I haven't been since the comet and the music and the kiss. Since the words on the wall. Since the back of the van. Since the kitchen and the laughter.

I'm not a survivor anymore. But I am alive.

"I'm awake," I whisper into the cold darkness.

I doze off. Somewhere in the night my shivering isn't enough to keep me awake anymore. But the sudden banging on the door is.

Directly behind me, separated by only inches of steel door, are clawing hands and shuffling feet. Gnashing teeth and hungry, dead eyes. I can feel the salty trails of my tears dried on my cheeks, making them feel stiff and strange. My body is achingly cold and angry from sitting in front of this door for so long. I can't run. I doubt I can fight. Even if I can, how many are there? One for sure, for now, but how many will follow? Given enough time, there will be enough to bring the door down and where will I go from there?

Light is building in the sky, telling me where east is. Taunting me with the knowledge that now means nothing to me. I'm sitting facing it, watching the warm glow grow and grow as the pounding behind me builds as well. Another set of hands has joined in. How many can the door hold? Not many, I imagine. The light is turning yellow, rays of the sun piercing the dark sky and falling on my face. In my eyes, blinding me. I wince against the light, reminded of my last moment out in the wild before they shut me in the van.

Then I'm on my feet, falling as my numb legs try to support my weight. I rise again, stumbling and crawling toward the edge of the building, looking for the perfect spot. A place where the skyline gives me a clear view toward my neighborhood. Toward a red brick building on 7th and Boren.

I pull the trowel from my pocket and shine it with my shirt as best I can. I spit on it again and again, moistening the dried blood that I try so hard not to think about. Some of it is the Risen's. Some of it is not. Finally it shines like new and I hope so hard it hurts my heart. This will work. This has to work.

I use the rays of the sun, reflecting them on the clean shine of the metal. I create the most erratic pattern I can manage. I'm not going for an SOS, I don't know Morse Code. All I can do is get someone's attention. I can only hope that I'm not too far away. That he's watching. That his sharp, unnerving eyes are enough to save me.

The moans at the door increase behind me. The sun's rays disappear behind a walking bridge between two nearby buildings. I drop the trowel by my side and I wonder if it was enough. If the Lost Boys will save me.

But when have I ever needed saving?

"Are you a Wendy?" I whisper to myself, scanning the low rooftops on the surrounding buildings. It's a long drop to every one of them. But is it too long? How would a person know unless they tried?

I take several steps back from the edge, bouncing on the balls of my feet. Then I crouch.

"Or are you a mutherfucking Tinkerbell?"

Following is
Chapter One of
Backs Against the Wall,
The next book in the Survival Series.
Coming in February 2014!

Chapter One

I may be a Tinkerbell, but I'm definitely Tink when she's trapped in the lamp gasping for her last breath, begging the world to believe and clap their friggin' hands. In essence, I cannot fly. I know it the second my foot leaves the ledge. I feel it when I go airborne. I've done this sort of jump enough to know my limits, to know when I'll get hurt and when I'll be fine, and I absolutely know it now.

It's too far.

I tuck and roll the best I can but gravity is unkind. I've gathered momentum, too much to be useful, just enough to be hurtful, and I tumble head over shoulders over side over elbows onto knees. I'm pretty sure I did a cartwheel back there somewhere, something I wish my mom could have seen. She spent hours with me in the backyard one sunny summer day trying to teach me how to do them. I always managed to land on my head. She eventually called it, telling me to give it a rest before I hurt something important. It's advice I wish I'd remembered back up on that higher roof. Now as the skin of my face is left somewhere 10 feet back, my right cheek having taken a hell of a blow on the rough tar rooftop, I also remember something else important.

I never liked Tinkerbell. She was a jealous jerk who deserved what she got and worse.

Finally I tumble to a stop on my back, smacking my head hard against the ground until I see stars.

"Ow," I mumble weakly.

I'm not sure what I'm complaining about. There's too much pain to inventory all at once. I'll have to take stock of my body one limb, muscle and burning abrasion at a time. This will take a while. But the good news is I have nothing but time. The zombies are still out there, very nearby I might add, and I have no clear idea of how I'm getting off this roof now that I worked so hard to get here. If I go inside this building, I'm going in blind and defenseless. I don't know what the situation is in there, if there even is one. Way my luck is going, there is. No doubt about it.

I move my legs. First the right, then the left. No breaks. Good news. There's a pulled muscle or two down there but nothing I can't handle. My arms are next. Right one, good. Left one—

"Holy Mary Mother of God Almighty." I grind out through gritted teeth as I roll back and forth on the ground trying to escape the pain. "Oh yeah, that's broken. Soooo broken."

My language goes far downhill from there. Jack and Jill tumbling down and breaking every bone along the merry way kind of downhill. I take a few deep breaths, vowing to never move my left arm again, and I test out the rest of me. Neck is good. That's a relief. Head is sore along with the face but I haven't begun vomiting, no dizziness, no blurred vision. Odds are I took a hard hit but no concussion. Ignoring the left arm (something I dare you to do someday. Go ahead, break it and pretend it never happened. Can't be done!) I'm alright. I'm mobile. I've got a snowball's chance in hell of surviving this. But I know I can't do it alone. Not with a broken arm and limited defenses.

I reach for my trowel, ready to take another shot at signaling for help despite my I-am-Wonder-Woman-I-need-no-man moment back there. Independence is great but real strength is being able to ask for help when you need it. And man oh man do I need it right now. I won't sit around wishing and hoping someone will save me but I do understand I have to keep trying to get help. I'm going to expose myself to the biggest, baddest gang out there if all goes according to this terrible, suicidal plan, so announcing myself to any other gang is really no big deal. Unless it's the cannibals. Screw those guys. I'd rather be zombie dinner than end up on their plate. At least the zombies can't feel feelings any more, making them sort of blameless. What's the cannibal's excuse? Crazy, that's what.

Unfortunately my trowel is no longer with me. I sit up, hugging my arm to my chest. I give out a groan but otherwise the pain is being handled internally. I broke it somewhere near the elbow because all I can feel is white hot pain in that area. I refuse to look at it though. I know I'll see bone and I can't handle that now. It's too real. If I see how truly awful, crazy, jacked up bad it is, I'll give up. I'll imagine it hurts worse than it already does and I'll assume I'm dead meat. I need denial to make it out of this alive.

I scan the rooftop for the trowel but it's MIA.

"Perfect."

Alright, no more calls for help. I wanted to do it alone and it looks like that's what I'll do. I stand up slowly, letting my skin stretch in new ways that tells me where more cuts and scrapes are. To be clear, by 'scrapes' I mean road burn. I mean sections of skin lost to the rooftop like it was trying to make a Joss suit it could wear. My thin Colony clothes are ripped wide open in several places making them nearly useless. I'm shivering again, something that's working wonders for my arm.

The way I see it I have two options. I'm in no condition to see The Hive today. They prey upon weakness and in my current state I am all weak sauce. I can go to Crenshaw to have him bandage me up or I can go to Ryan. That's it with that second option. No real benefits, no promise of help or healing. Just Ryan. One choice is smart, one is emotional and I hate, loathe and despise emotional. But can you imagine which option I'm considering the hardest?

I make my way to the door leading off this roof. I'm relieved when it opens easily. I was worried it would be locked as so many these days are. Like my water sources all are. Not that it seems to matter since people still break into them and rob me blind. My temper flares, fueling my aching body with the steam it needs to get down the long flight of stairs, through the seemingly endless corridors and out into the growing morning light.

There are Risen everywhere.

They haven't spotted me yet. In fact, most are heading toward the building I jumped from, probably answering the siren call of the other Risen still pounding on a door to the rooftop to get to me. But in my current state, openly broken and bleeding all over the road, it won't take long for them to catch my scent. As it is I'm bleeding steadily from my arm onto the pavement.

I turn quickly, taking off at a fast pace as I pull the hem of my shirt up high until my left arm is cradled in it against my chest. I ball up the excess fabric in my right fist as much as I can to pin my injured arm in place. I feel tears sting my eyes as what feels like sandpaper against raw nerve screams from my elbow through my entire body. I have to bite my lip to keep from crying out. To keep from basically waving to the Risen and saying, 'Hey! Over here! Breakfast is served!'

With my shoddy makeshift sling in painful place, I run. I book it as fast as my sore, sorrowful legs will carry me. I dart down alleys trying to avoid Risen but they're everywhere. I can't get away from them and I find eventually that my best bet is to run right down the center of the street dodging them when I have to. Hands reach for me, mouths snap toward me, but it's nothing I'm not used. I tune it out and focus up. But all the focus in the world can't make me fast enough to outrun this city.

A Risen tackles me as I try to dart out of the way. She grabs onto different parts of my body as she slides down the side of me while I try to continue to run. I'm using denial again, pretending I absolutely do not have a 130 lbs zombie hanging from my waist right now. Eventually she slips down far enough that I think I'll escape but she grabs my leg and we both hit the pavement hard. Luckily I'm able to roll onto my back. It's good news for my busted arm, my face and my life. Never, never, never ever let a Risen get your back. You can't fight them off, you can't hold them off. If they get ahold of you from behind in any way, especially pinning you to the ground, we'll all miss you and say lovely words at your funeral because you're dead.

She grabs onto the waist of my pants, trying to use it to climb up my body but the best she gets is pulling the loose material down my hips slightly. I roll as far as I can away from her then I swing back toward her where she rests on my leg, bringing my free knee up. I put all of my force and momentum behind it. I'm able to crack her right in the face, stunning her enough to scurry back, clearing my feet from her grasp. I'm in no condition to fight her any more than this so I roll over on my good arm and use it to help hoist me up onto my feet. My nearly useless sling is now completely useless so I cradle my left arm with my right and I run.

I run until my lungs burn. I run until my legs are rubber. I run until the Risen have thinned and I have a chance to stop for two seconds to try to catch my breath so I can run some more. The only good thing about today so far is that it's just that; day. I can see. I have landmarks to tell me where I'm heading and whether or not I'm running in blind circles surrounded by a sea of Risen. I'm still really far from home. Maybe too far. I might have to take up residence in one of these buildings soon. Definitely before nightfall.

I know I need to get moving but I feel like I can't. I feel it in my entire bitter body. I haven't slept, I haven't eaten and I'm fading fast. I need water soon for sure and a bandage or fifty would be nice too.

"You don't want to stop here." a voice calls quietly from down a dark alley nearby.

I jump to attention, nearly leaping out of my ruined skin.

"This is The Eleven's territory." he continues. "They'll eat you alive."

"Are you one of them?" I demand, sounding fiercer than I feel.

He's nothing but a motionless shadow wrapped in darkness. A vague form inked in black on black paper.

"No."

"Then you shouldn't be here either. Why don't we both leave and no one has to get hurt?"

"I thought you wanted me to come."

I scowl, confused. "What?"

"Your signal."

The trowel. The light.

"You saw it?"

A figure steps out slowly, emerging from the shadows by degrees. Tall, blond hair. Kind of gangly. But it's his eyes that I notice more than anything. They're razor sharp, slicing my momentary strong façade to shreds. He sees it. He sees how broken I am. He sees it because he sees everything.

Trent.

About the Author

I grew up in Eugene, Oregon (Go Ducks!) where I met and married my best friend. Now he, our son, our pitbull and I go where the Air Force tells us. Luckily a girl can write zombie lit anywhere. I love telling a good, fun story with female characters who are strong and independent but who have a soft spot for a guy who can make them laugh, no matter what the situation. It's good to know you can survive the apocalypse on your own, but it's even better to know someone has your back.

Made in the USA
Lexington, KY
07 June 2017